WOLF OF BLOOD

USA TODAY BESTSELLING AUTHOR
AMELIA SHAW

CHAPTER 1
TALIA

After the incident with the flaming hot hypnotist in the alleyway, aka. Galen banned me from going into town. Especially alone.

I'd been ordered to stay on pack grounds, with the proviso that I could help the pack, if I wanted to. Which, of course, I did. Considering how many people were trying to kill me, Galen's over-protectiveness was fine by me.

The pack Alpha, Galen's father, had woken up in hospital after he'd collapsed and refused to stay there once he realized where he was. So, he was home resting once more.

Galen wanted me close at hand, so he moved me into the Alpha's house and into a spare bedroom. That made my task of finding a job to keep myself occupied a lot easier. I made the Alpha meals and cleaned the house for him, much like I would have done for my own dad. Before he was killed.

I found it a surprisingly satisfying job to make sure the older Alpha was comfortable. He was nothing like the Alpha from my old pack. Galen's dad was a nice man, and so much gentler than anyone I'd been used to, from my old life. He spoke to me, and others, with respect. In my experience, that was rare in a man of his bloodline.

After a slightly stilted start, we'd fallen into a comfortable daily rhythm.

"Talia?" the Alpha called out from his bedroom.

I raced over to his room and hung in the doorway. "Yes, Alpha?"

"Could you go up to the Grayson house and get our weekly quota of eggs? They're the farm on the corner with the white picket fence."

I smiled at him, admiring the way he always made my job that little bit easier with extra details about the people and properties that were still unfamiliar to me.

"Of course!" I replied, pulling off my rubber gloves. He'd caught me in the middle of doing the dishes. I was always especially happy to do anything that got me out of the house when I could.

I was grateful for the protection Galen's pack, and Galen himself, afforded me. But my wolf was dying for a run and itching to get out in the fresh air.

I grabbed a sweater because the skies were darkening, and it looked like rain.

"Be back soon," I called toward the Alpha's bedroom, before opening the front door.

I inhaled deeply, smelling the moisture in the air. It was going to pour down. And soon.

I headed toward the edge of town, looking for the house with the white picket fence.

A few of the pack members that I passed gave me hesitant smiles, and I waved in response. They weren't sure about me, that was clear, and I understood why. I wasn't just unfamiliar, or a stranger like Darius. I'd been a member of an enemy pack that had recently attacked and killed some of their men.

I was grateful they were being as nice as they were. After all, if it had been the reverse and they were the stranger in my old pack... well, let's just say I was relieved not to be stoned in the street.

I wrapped my cardigan around my body tighter as a cool breeze whipped around me. The storm was truly on its way. I hurried a little faster along the road.

When I spotted the white picket fence in front of the house on the corner, I jogged up and knocked on the door, then retraced my steps back to stand by the front gate. The people in this town were suspicious of strangers and I didn't want to upset anyone by being on their property without permission.

There was the distinctive scent of chickens and they were clucking, though I couldn't see them anywhere. They must be out back in the yard, or down the side of the house.

An older woman with a suspicious look on her face opened the front door and walked out onto the porch, holding a carton of eggs. "Are you here on behalf of the Alpha?"

"Yes," I said. Everyone knew I was staying with Galen's father. "He sent me down to fetch some eggs. Looks like you already knew that."

I softened my words with a small smile.

She strolled toward the gate, her long gray hair blowing around her face. "The whole town's talking about you. You're the girl Galen stole, then saved from the Northwood pack."

I wrapped my arms around myself. "Yeah. They forced me out of my pack and told me to I had to leave the state." I shrugged. "But Galen stopped me, and now I'm here."

The woman stood on the other side of the fence. Her keen gaze roamed over me, and I remained still, allowing her to look.

I had nothing to hide. Quite the opposite. I wanted these people to know me and learn to trust me. I wasn't here to hurt them, and eventually they'd work that out.

She finally handed me the eggs, and when I checked inside the carton, several of them still had little chook feathers attached.

"You look like a good girl. If you need anything else, especially for the Alpha, you come ask for Joan. Okay?"

"Thank you, Joan." I clutched the eggs to my belly. "I appreciate it."

"You better go." She nodded behind me. "The storm's almost on us, and it looks like a big one."

I gave her one last grateful smile, then turned tail and headed back in the direction of the Alpha's house.

I was about fifty feet away from my destination when someone yelled out. "Talia! Talia!"

I stopped dead in my tracks. I knew that voice. Female. Familiar. No way. It couldn't be.

I whirled around, looking for the face that went with that voice.

"Talia!"

Oh, my God.

"Celia!" I gasped when my best friend's face popped out of the shadows near the tree she was hiding behind in a neighboring yard.

I looked around, checking that no one was watching me as I slowly made my way into the yard and over to Celia.

I leaned against the tree, with my back to the trunk, so that it would look like I was simply taking a break on my walk.

"Celia? What are you doing here?" I hissed.

Galen's Betas ran security around the pack all day and all night. How had she gotten through undetected?

"I had to. I needed to speak to you." She kept her voice to a whisper. "I'm so glad you're okay. The Alpha's increased the directive. He told everyone in the pack to kill you on sight. He said that some of his Betas were killed in a fight outside of town and it had something to do with you. I got so worried that you'd be next."

I closed my eyes and leaned my head back against the tree trunk. "Yeah, they came for me and tried to kill me. We had to deal with them."

There was a beat of silence, then Celia asked, "What do you mean, we? Who killed the Betas?"

"Galen," I whispered, glancing around once more to make sure no one was looking our way. "The Alpha's son."

"Are you okay? I mean, have they hurt you?"

I shook my head. "No, not at all. He hasn't hurt me. None of them have. They've been… well, he's… protected me."

"Listen, Talia." Celia forged on as if I hadn't just told her that an enemy Alpha and his pack were protecting me. "You need to get away from all of this. Get in your dad's car at night fall and drive across the state borders. Get as far away from here as you can."

I frowned at her insistent words, and her tone was even more frantic.

"Why, Celia? What's going on?"

"Maddox is planning something terrible for you, Talia. He… he… You need to leave. He's going to kill you. And you don't deserve it. You've done nothing wrong."

That wasn't news to me. My own pack had tried to kill me a couple of times now. The shock factor was still high, but the facts were clear. My old pack wanted me dead, and Galen's pack offered a safe haven. For now.

"I know I haven't," I said. "They killed my dad, Celia. Right in front of me. Then Maddox rejected our mating bond and threw me out of the pack. Do they really have to kill me as well? They already destroyed my life."

My throat tightened with hot tears, and I stopped talking. Everything was such a mess and every time I thought about what had happened in the past few weeks, it just seemed like a terrible nightmare.

"I'm so sorry, Talia." Celia's voice was so low I almost didn't hear it.

I turned to answer her, but she was gone. I blinked a couple of times at her quick disappearance.

A man I didn't recognize, with long dark hair, stepped around the side of the house. "Can I help you?"

"No. I'm sorry," I said, still clutching the eggs. "I just had to stop and catch my breath. I was on my way back to the Alpha's house, from Joan's."

He nodded but didn't introduce himself. "You better get back then. The heavens are about to open."

"Yes, sir." I put my head down and hurried back into the road just as the first drops of cold rain hit my face.

Hopefully, Celia had gotten away without being discovered.

I rushed up the porch steps and opened the front door of the Alpha's home, then turned and looked back down the road. Celia had been dressed, so that meant she hadn't gotten here in wolf form. She must have driven and parked nearby, then walked over to find me.

The girl was crazy. What she'd done was such a dangerous move. Galen's pack were on high alert, and they wouldn't have thought twice about taking Celia down if they thought she posed a threat.

Would she be able to get away safely?

What if they caught her?

Lightning cracked in the sky above, and I shut the front door against the gust of chilly wind that blew against the house.

"Brrr... It's cold out there," I said to the empty kitchen, trying to put my worry about Celia aside as I placed the eggs on the countertop.

The Alpha called out, "Talia. Is that you?"

"It's me, Alpha. I've got the eggs. Would you like some lunch?"

"No, thank you. But you make some for yourself."

I smiled at the generosity of the man. He wasn't hungry, and yet he was offering me his food.

"Thank you, Alpha."

My stomach was in knots. Celia had risked her life to come here and track me down. Against her Alpha's wishes.

Against *Maddox*.

She was a friend, in the truest sense of the word.

But the message she'd come to deliver was one I already knew, so I wasn't sure why she'd risked her life to tell me that. My old Alpha had ordered our people to kill me on sight and confirmed that I was being punished for my father's mistakes. So, was there a more urgent message I needed to hear?

Had something made Celia more panicked? Was Maddox himself now coming for me? What had changed to ramp up the danger?

I didn't know, and I needed to talk to Galen to hash things out with him. But he was working with the pack today.

I spent the afternoon on autopilot, cleaning the Alpha's kitchen and making a dinner that I hoped everyone would enjoy.

When Galen finally arrived home at the end of the day, I

practically sagged with relief. I could talk to him. Try and make sense of everything whirling around in my head.

"Hey," he called out, nodding at me as he pulled off his gray sweater. He shook the rain from his hair before he tucked the longer strands behind his ear. "Food smells good. How was your day?"

"Can I talk to you?" I asked without preamble, shivering unexpectedly in his company.

He stared at me as though assessing my query for hidden meaning, and then nodded. "Give me a minute to check on my dad, then we'll talk."

"Okay."

Galen disappeared and I poured myself a glass of water to make the time go faster, then turned on the oven and put in the garlic bread I'd prepared earlier.

When Galen got back, his lips curved into a soft smile. "He's in much better shape with you around."

I tried to smile but shivered instead. "I like being here, Galen. Your dad's nice."

And it made me feel useful being here. The Alpha couldn't walk anywhere except to the bathroom, so making sure he had water, food and blankets, and anything else he needed, felt like a valuable contribution to the household.

I wasn't sure how they'd handled things before I got here, but leaving him home alone all day didn't seem like a good thing to do to him.

"Now, what's wrong?" Galen asked, pulling up a stool and sitting at the kitchen counter.

He stared at me, waiting, and my bravery shrunk. So I diverted, fast.

"Are you hungry?" I asked. "I made dinner."

"I am, but I want you to tell me what's got you shivering so much. I've seen you face death a couple of times now, and you weren't this shaken up."

I took a sip of water, then laughed a little at his expression. It was nice to know that he didn't think I was weak, even though that was how I saw myself. "You're right. I think it was just seeing Celia that got to me."

"Celia?" Galen repeated, his eyebrows drawing together.

"Yeah. Celia." A wave of sadness passed over me, threatening to suck me down into the depths of darkness.

I shook myself and straightened my spine. My pack had come to kill me not once, but twice now. I'd survived, and I would survive whatever else was coming my way. Now was not the time to break down.

"Celia is one of my best friends. She has been since childhood. She snuck over here, and hid, so she could talk to me."

Galen stood quickly, the stool legs scraping on the kitchen tiles as he did.

"One of your old pack was here?" His tone was shocked. "She got through our security without detection?"

I nodded. "Yeah, I suppose."

Galen crossed his arms over his chest. His expression darkened. "Well, that's not good. I'll talk to my guys. But what did she want?"

I swallowed hard, readying myself to tell him the truth. "She came to warn me. She said that my ex-fiancé, Maddox, is planning to come and kill me."

And although that wasn't a new piece of information, it was what Galen would do with such news that worried me.

CHAPTER 2
GALEN

"Your fated mate is planning to kill you?" I asked, not sure I'd heard correctly.

Did she mean Maddox, himself, or did their pack have a new plan I needed to know about?

Her face hardened, her eyes flashing. "He's not my mate."

"I meant—"

"No. I know what you meant," Talia snapped. "But Maddox and I aren't mated. We never even had sex. And even though we were fated..."

She stopped talking and swallowed hard, her throat working.

I nodded in acceptance of what she said. Acceptance... and sympathy. I couldn't imagine being rejected by a fated mate. Not only that, but being betrayed by the one person who was supposed to be your soul mate. The ultimate betrayal.

"I misspoke," I admitted, watching her carefully to see if she was about to break.

Not Talia. She was strong. She raised her chin and faced me squarely.

"Okay," I said. "So let me get this straight. One of your friends from your old pack risked her life by sneaking through our perimeter to warn you that Maddox is out to kill you."

We already knew that the pack had orders to kill Talia on sight, of course. But this felt different. There was something more personal and determined in this latest development.

Talia nodded, then leaned heavily on the counter like she couldn't stand upright without support any longer. "It's never going to end, Galen. Is it? They're always going to hunt me. Come for me. And they're not going to stop, until I'm dead."

Tears tracked down her cheeks and she lifted her hand to wipe them away. "Celia told me that I needed to just get in my Dad's car and leave. Do you think I should?"

I gaped at her. "You want to leave?"

I was shocked she'd even suggested it, but why was I? I shouldn't be. When I found her, she'd been running away, so why wouldn't she want to continue that path now?

Anger and frustration burned in my chest and my breathing hitched in my throat. I really didn't want her to go. The very idea turned me cold as ice, and angry at the Fates that were forcing her to choose a path I didn't agree with.

"No! I don't *want* to leave." She shook her head. "This town is my home, now, but Celia could be right. Maybe it's better to run away to fight another day. I don't know. What if my being here endangers your pack?"

"My pack is strong, Talia," I said, infusing confidence into my tone. She was right to be concerned on that front, but I was right, too. We *were* strong. "And you live here, now. If you don't want to leave, then stay."

I could protect her. My pack would too, under my instructions. Even though some of my Betas thought I was nuts for offering to help Talia, they'd do as I instructed.

"I'll never be safe. Here or anywhere," she whispered. "Would you help me if I decided to leave, Galen? Run with me to the border? Do you think we'd make it?"

"In wolf form?"

She was talking about five hundred miles.

"No," I said, honestly.

I could run for days in wolf form and Talia was a fast shifter, but even so it was too far, with too strong an enemy. If they snuck up on us at night and killed her, I would never forgive myself.

She released a tiny sob. "Then I'll drive, like Celia suggested. Take my dad's car. I'll go tonight."

"No, you won't," I told her firmly. "You'll stay here tonight. Safe. Under the Alpha's roof. Then tomorrow, I'll fix this."

I could feel a plan forming in the back of my mind, but it wasn't one I was ready to share yet.

"How?" Her eyes were huge and wide as she stared at me. "How are you going to fix it?"

There was only one way. "Do you trust me, Talia?"

She nodded. "I do."

My ribs squeezed tightly as pride blossomed somewhere deep inside, dark and hidden.

"Then let me organize what I need to do with my Betas, and tomorrow, I'll deal with it."

Talia nodded, wiping away a few more tears that had strayed onto her beautiful cheeks.

She didn't ask any more questions, which was likely an advantage of her being raised to be an Alpha's mate. Talia's instincts led her to follow directions and inherently trust a man that had my bloodlines.

But there was a flip side to that trust and submission. It meant that the Alpha in me wanted to protect her even more.

"You want some dinner now? I'll take some in to your dad in a moment." Her shoulders slumped as though we'd had a fight and she'd lost, which was quite the opposite of what had happened.

"Yes, please. Tell me how Dad's been today for you."

After she delivered dinner to Dad, Talia chatted with me easily about my father while we ate. The food was tasty and showcased her talents in the kitchen. Eventually, I excused myself to talk to my Betas and prepare for the next day.

I ripped into them about our security lines, not caring when they all showed shock and dismay. After all, a female wolf from a neighboring enemy pack should never have been able to get onto our territory without detection. And especially not to be able to reach Talia so easily. The very idea of it galled me. Thank God she'd been a friendly, and not one sent to kill Talia.

I informed my Betas of my plan and what I was willing to do to save our pack from future fights, and hopefully prevent Talia from losing her life. The guys were ready to string me up when I voiced my thoughts, and they called me every crazy name under the sun, but I wouldn't be moved.

There was only one way of saving Talia, and I was going to do it. Whatever it took.

THE NEXT MORNING, I didn't tell my dad where I was going or what I was planning. There was no need to worry him until I got back. Then, once he heard what I'd done, he could tear me a new one.

Assuming I survived, of course.

I woke up early, dressed into some old, shifting clothes, and left the house.

I'd only taken a few steps from the front porch when I heard her voice.

"Galen! Wait!"

Talia came running out of the front door in nothing more than her black panties and a tank top that showed her sexy midriff. No bra.

Her breasts bounced as she ran down the stairs and her nipples peaked against the material of her top in the cold morning air.

"Where are you going?" she asked as she crossed her arms over her chest, shielding her nipples from the cold. And my view.

I straightened my spine and hardened myself against the desire sweeping my body. "I'm going to have a little talk with Maddox."

"You're..." Her mouth dropped open. "You're going to... *talk* to Maddox?"

I nodded. "There's only one way to save you, Talia."

My Betas knew what to do if I didn't come back. They had a strategy now, and I'd named Markus as my successor. I'd made note of it on the papers in my room in case anyone had questions.

I wasn't ready to die, but I wasn't going to stand by and let Talia die either.

Her eyes filled with tears and her bottom lip quivered. She knew me better than I'd thought. "You're going to challenge him."

"Yes, I am."

He was an Alpha's son. So was I. He had fury driving him, but I had more. I had Talia.

"Galen. No... please..."

The time for talking was done. I stripped off my t-shirt and pushed my jeans down my thighs, letting my wolf rise up inside my soul and tear through my human body.

Part of me wished I could grab and kiss her, take her taste with me into battle. But if I stopped to touch her now, I wasn't sure I'd be able to fight afterwards. I needed every bit of unsatisfied lust to fuel my rage.

Instead, I stood before her as my large black wolf, set on protecting the woman before me, then turned tail and ran—across my own pack lines and into enemy territory.

I kept running as the sun rose over the horizon, lighting the way. There were buildings up ahead, and houses. I made my way through the streets, the bubbling of my anger boiling through me.

Then I stopped, right in the middle of their town. I shifted back to human, my body hot and slick with sweat. My chest heaved with each breath I took, and my wolf howled inside my mind, craving violence.

Women stopped to stare at my nakedness, then rushed past me. An old guy gaped at me from the side of the road.

"I want your Alpha!" I bellowed into the street. "Now!"

A group of men marched down the street toward me.

I stood firm and faced them, clenching my hands into fists. "I am Galen... future Alpha of the Long Claw Pack."

I scanned the group as they surged forward and locked eyes with a guy about my age, perhaps a little younger. He had a soft, pretty-boy type of face and it turned my stomach to look at him. I knew who he was by my reaction. I didn't need it confirmed.

"Maddox. I challenge you."

The group of six men stopped before me and an older man, with graying hair and a huge build, stalked forward. "I'm the Alpha of this pack, not Maddox. You want a challenge? Challenge me, pup."

I lifted my chin. "If I win, you leave Talia and my pack alone."

He dismissed my words with a flick of his hand.. "You gotta win first."

He began tugging at his clothes as though I would be fighting him.

I shook my head. "I'm not fighting a man older than my father. I want Maddox. Is he too cowardly to step up?"

The pretty-faced man I'd spotted earlier rushed forward. He was taller than the Alpha and stood at the right hand of his father. "No one calls me a coward. You want me? Then you get me."

My gaze locked on him, and a growl rolled through my chest. This was the fuckwit who'd left Talia untouched. The man who'd rejected her and tossed her aside when all she'd wanted was to serve him.

Asshole. You never deserved someone like her.

The Alpha thrust out his arm, stopping his son and never taking his eyes off me. "No. I'm the Alpha of this pack. I'm the one who gave the order. Talia had her chance to get out of the state. She didn't take it. That decision and the consequence falls on her, not us."

I clenched my teeth. "I want the threat taken off her."

The Alpha began to strip. "Boy, if you win, only then we will talk terms. But you won't win."

The growl that ripped through the old Alpha as he shifted was one of feral, nasty strength.

I responded in kind. Maddox would not step up now that his father had called it. I was already naked, so I quickly shifted to my wolf form, shook out my fur, and planted my paws firmly in the road.

We were evenly matched in size and weight. This fight would not be easy to win.

It might possibly be a fight to the death.

He launched at me, his snapping teeth, aiming for my throat.

I sprung back, out of his reach, and then twisted on my paws to face him again. This time, when he launched, I was ready.

His huge maw with vicious teeth snapped together an inch from my neck as I jerked away. I lunged in to score a bite on his shoulder. I ripped through his thick fur to expose the flesh beneath, and held on, tasting blood. It fired my senses, that taste, and I shook him, hard, before letting go.

He yelped and limped backward. Then we were on each other again, biting and growling and swiping at each other.

The sounds we made must have been horrendous for those watching, and vaguely I wondered where Talia was right now.

Then I put her out of my head, because I had to concentrate on staying alive.

I had never fought someone so evenly matched. My usual size and weight advantage was nullified against this enormous Alpha.

He caught me on the back leg and held on. It took all my strength to throw him off. I backed away, shaking my head to re-orient myself.

That one hurt. A lot.

I spared a glance downward to see blood gushing from a huge wound on my leg and another gash on my hip.

When had he got me there?

Blood was everywhere. His *and* mine.

I couldn't worry about injuries now. I glared at my enemy, noting the red fire of blood lust in his eyes. My lip curled up, and I snarled, battle-lust raging through my body and infusing me with power and energy, despite the blood loss.

His shoulders bunched as he readied to leap at me again. I held my ground, lowered my head, and charged him first.

I caught him round the neck, and I dropped my weight to the ground, pulling him down with me. I locked my jaw, refusing to give up, even under a torrent of scratches and scrabbling all over my body as he fought to release from my grip.

If I let go now, I was a dead wolf.

From this position, I could only see one of his eyes, and it was full of rage and a hint of fear.

Then he stopped scrabbling as the rage dissipated and the fear in his expression grew. He arched his neck further, which would allow me to finish him off if I so desired. It was a classic sign of defeat. He was signaling to me, and to anyone watching, that I had won this battle.

The Alpha was conceding the fight.

I detached my locked jaw from around his throat, tasting his blood as it ran down my gullet and fighting the urge to give him one last shake and finish him off. This bastard had tried to kill Talia. He deserved death in return. But I needed to back off and, let the negotiations begin. That wouldn't happen if I killed him.

It was done. I'd won. And Talia would finally be safe.

I let go of my wolf, needing to withdraw from the red haze of anger and adrenaline. I slid back into my human body with exhaustion, feeling barely alive as I climbed to my feet and stared around.

My gaze locked onto Maddox, who stood as still as a statue, as if he was shocked at the outcome.

Blood poured from my wounds, but I ignored it.

"Let's talk terms," I said.

CHAPTER 3
TALIA

I couldn't believe Galen had left to fight my old Alpha. What if he was killed? My chest filled with dread at the thought.

I ran back inside and dressed. The sun was barely up and much of the town was likely still asleep.

Not me. Instead, I paced and worried, until I couldn't bear my whirling thoughts any longer. But what could I do? I couldn't stop the fight, and if it didn't go Galen's way, where could I go?

Tears fell down my cheeks until I became so angry at my own frustration, I scrubbed at my face under the kitchen sink tap. Then I took a few deep breaths to calm myself, before I went to ask Galen's dad if he needed anything.

Luckily for me, the Alpha gave me a list of errands, which was a useful distraction. I ran from one house to another, collecting food and dropping things off as he'd requested.

I didn't tell the Alpha where Galen was, feigning complete ignorance when he asked if I knew where his son had run off to so early. I didn't see any of the Betas along the route. They were likely already working, or on patrol. They were probably avoiding me too, because after all, I was the reason their Alpha-to-be was putting his life at risk.

My stomach was completely tight with tension. I couldn't eat. I could hardly breathe. Galen, my protector, my captor, the man who had become my friend... he was, quite possibly, in the fight of his life right now. For me.

Was he hurt? Had he been killed?

What would happen to me, and to this pack, if something happened to him? It wasn't like Galen's dad could miraculously make himself well and jump out of bed to take over leadership once again.

The not knowing was the worst possible thing, and by the time my errands were done, all I could imagine was the worst outcome.

What if Galen never came back?

I rushed back to the house, put away the food I'd collected for the Alpha, then went to the bathroom to have a quick shower. I felt somehow unclean and even though I knew water couldn't wash away my worry, I couldn't resist cleaning myself from top to toe under the hot spray.

If Galen died, then I would surrender to my old pack. I didn't want anyone else getting hurt on my account and with Galen gone, who would keep this pack safe?

I wanted to live—0f course, I did—but not at the cost of anyone else's life. Especially those who had tried so hard to help me.

I scrubbed my flesh hard, from the soles of my feet to the scalp on the top of my head. But everywhere on my body was itchy and aching in a strange way.

Oh, please let this not be a premonition of any sort. Or if it is, please be a good one.

I wanted Galen home, now. I wasn't sure how it had happened so quickly, but Galen had become someone I trusted. Someone I cared about.

Once I was raw and clean, I dried myself and dressed, then walked outside and sat on the front step of the porch.

And I waited.

All day, I waited, moving off the porch only to make the Alpha some lunch and clean up after, before returning to my watching post on the porch.

If Galen had won the challenge, wouldn't he have returned straight away? It was close to dinner time now and the streets were empty of people.

If he'd lost, would Maddox's pack have taken immediate vengeance? Was that why there was no one around? Should I be readying myself to head back to my old home and hand myself in to whatever dreadful fate awaited me there?

"Oh God, what should I do?"

I jumped to my feet, biting my lip so hard I tasted blood. I considered my options. Should I try to find one of his Betas? Markus, maybe? He'd help me, surely? Would he run with me to the pack lines and see if we could find out what had happened to Galen?

Just when I was about to throw all caution to the wind and try to track him down myself, a large black wolf appeared in my vision, trotting down the street toward me. No, trotting wasn't accurate. He was limping down the street.

Limping quite badly, in fact.

It was Galen. No one else was that big or strong. Besides, I would know him anywhere, whether in wolf or human form.

He came straight toward me, and I rushed to meet him.

"Galen."

He was alive. My eyes filled with tears of relief.

Blood matted his fur, and I rushed back to the house to open the door and let him in.

"Come. Quickly," I said, gesturing to him.

Galen hurried towards the door, but he grimaced with every step.

"Everything okay?" the Alpha called out from the bedroom. "Do I smell blood?"

"All good. No problem," I called back, then motioned for Galen to follow me. "It's...uh... my monthly... you know."

My cheeks heated. I couldn't believe I'd just said that, but nothing else came to mind to explain the scent of Galen's injuries.

"All right. Sorry, didn't mean to pry," came the Alpha's muffled reply.

"Come to my bedroom," I whispered to Galen. "I'll get the first aid kit."

Galen limped down the hallway, bloody footprints trailing behind him. I grabbed everything I could find to help him: bandages, water bottles, disinfectant, needle and thread, cloths.

Then I raced down the hallway to my room, where Galen, completely naked in his human form, sat on my bed, swaying with exhaustion and blood loss.

"Hey..." He groaned as he pressed a hand to his head.

"You okay?" I asked, shutting the door behind me.

He was covered in so much blood, it looked painted on. Red was splashed over his face and down his chest.

"Yeah, I'm okay. A few injuries, but mostly I just need a shower."

I held up my supplies, trying hard not to look too long at the incredible body before me.

The one sitting on my bed.

Every time I saw Galen naked, he took my breath away with the strength and beauty of him. Even now, dirty and streaked with blood, he was damn beautiful.

"Do you need any stitches? Can I help you with any of your injuries?" I'd patched up my dad enough times after fights to know how to do most first aid. Especially on a wolf with a high pain tolerance and fast healing power.

"Ah, yeah." He turned to the side. "I think my back needs a little attention, and my leg. Near my ankle."

I dropped to my knees on the ground before him, keeping my head bent to stare at his ankle and foot.

The flesh had been mauled and blood still gushed out of the wound onto the floor beneath him. The pool of red was beginning to grow. I needed to stop that bleeding, fast. God knew how much he'd already lost, getting back here.

"This is gonna need stitches."

"Can you do it?"

I didn't raise my head, knowing what I would come eye to eye with if I tried to look up at him. I wasn't mature enough for that today. Nope. No way.

"I can."

"Then please do."

He extended his leg to give me full access and I got to it, washing away any grime with water, then applying the disinfectant before using the needle and thread to sew the flesh back together. It was a rough but passable job. Galen inhaled sharply above me while I sewed, but he didn't make any other sound.

When I was done, I added a waterproof covering, then bandaged up the wound and put some clips on to hold it all together.

I hopped to my feet without staring at his groin, an almost

impossible feat. The heat of my desire for him settled deep in my belly, and my breath kept hitching in my throat.

"Your ankle's done. Can I look at your back now?"

He nodded, not speaking, but twisted away so I could check out the scratches and teeth marks on his back. The skin was a mess, but it would heal. There was one gash over his hip deep enough to show flesh and bone but I wasn't sure if stitches were needed or not. It wasn't bleeding anymore. I cleaned that wound out, and added a few butterfly sutures and a waterproof dressing to hold it together. It didn't seem to need more than that, and with Galen's healing, it would hopefully not take too long to mend.

I studied his back some more. "Gee whiz. Did Maddox do all this to you?"

He huffed out a laugh. "Wimp wouldn't fight me. This was his father."

A chill coursed down my spine. "You fought the Alpha?"

How had he survived that encounter?

Galen turned back to face me and this time, I couldn't help but notice the way his cock lay thick and heavy against his thigh. My stomach clenched and I lifted my gaze up to his with effort.

"Yeah. Why?" he asked.

"Oh, because he's... very tough." I swallowed hard and walked away from him. "I don't think you need stitches for anything on your back, but I could look again after a shower. I can disinfect it then, too. Do you need help getting in and out?"

Galen got to his feet and his cock wasn't flaccid anymore.

Wow. Even with all that pain...

"No. I'm fine. But if you could look over my back again afterward, that would be great."

"Use my shower," I said, indicating to the ensuite I had,

thanks to Galen giving me his room. He was sleeping in a spare room. "I'll clean up and be here when you get out."

There were several pools of blood on the floor and the blankets on the bed would need a wash now.

"Thanks." He limped to the bathroom.

I hurried to the kitchen to gather paper towels and more water, my face aflame. The water was running in the bathroom and I tried to slow down my heart rate.

He'd fought my old Alpha and survived.

No one I knew, or had even heard of for that matter, had fought our Alpha and lived to tell the tale. He was a monster of a man, and his wolf was equally vicious.

So, what had happened to him?

Had Galen killed him?

Maybe I didn't want to know the answer to that one.

I hurried to clean up, stripping my bed and putting the blankets and sheets straight into the washing machine. I mopped up the blood on the floor and put the water down an outside drain, then went back in and remade my bed with sheets and blankets I found in a cabinet.

When the shower finally turned off and the door to the ensuite opened to reveal a still very naked but much less bloody Galen, my heart soared.

"How are you feeling?" I asked, then swallowed the excited squeal rising in my throat.

He pushed wet hair off his face, his naked torso rippling with muscle. "A lot better, actually."

He slung the towel around his waist, low on his hips, and limped forward. "Can you check my back again? It's still sore."

"Yeah, of course." I rushed forward, stepping behind him while he was still standing. I set my hands to his flesh, pressing my palms flat and spreading my fingers wide.

The strength of his body radiated out in a wave. I quivered, then clenched my teeth, hard, forcing whatever that feeling was to retreat. Now was not the time for anything other than caregiving. Galen had been hurt, because of my presence here in his pack, and I needed to focus.

After taking a long, slow breath, I moved my hands down his spine to the indent of his lower back, checking marks and wounds as I went.

He was hot to the touch, his skin smooth beneath my fingertips.

"They look okay," I whispered, pressing against the claw marks on his shoulder, then checking the one at the base of his spine near his hip where the wound was a lot deeper. The butterfly sutures seemed to have survived the shower and were holding well. "Can I put some antiseptic cream on these ones on your back?"

As long as the gashes didn't become infected, Galen's wolf genetics would step in and heal him quickly.

"Yeah." His voice was deep and gravelly. "That'd be great."

I rushed over to my pile of supplies and grabbed the white tube. Then, with shaking hands, I squirted some of the cream onto my fingertips and applied it to the remaining wounds.

"Is that okay?" I asked as he stiffened beneath my touch.

"Yeah. Just cold." His voice was still croaky.

I covered all the claw marks with the antiseptic.

"I think I'm done," I whispered.

"Thanks." He swayed a little on his feet. "I think I need to sit down again."

Crap! I knew he'd lost too much blood.

"Of course!" I said, grabbing his arm and tugging him across to the bed.

When he sat, I climbed onto the bed as well, sitting

behind him cross-legged and facing his shoulder, so that if he fell, I could make sure he landed on the mattress and not the floor.

"Are you okay?" I asked, placing my hand on his arm.

He nodded but didn't turn toward me.

I coughed to clear my throat, my gaze sweeping over his incredible muscles. I wanted to touch him more, caress him. Learn each groove and curve of him.

But I had a burning question I needed an answer to. "Did you, uh… kill the Alpha?"

Galen turned his head, his eyes blazing with his wolf as he stared at me.

I gasped, unable to look away.

"No. I didn't."

"Then what happened?" I whispered.

He'd come home after being at the other pack all day and considering that an Alpha's challenge usually meant a fight to the death, Galen's injuries were quite mild, really.

"I fought him and won. But I refused to kill him. Instead, I made him concede. Then Maddox and I talked terms while some of their other pack members carried their injured leader away somewhere."

"Terms?" My gaze dropped to his mouth as he spoke, and it took a moment to process what he'd said. "You talked terms with Maddox?"

"Yes. You're free." He said it like a simple statement of fact. "You're safe. They won't come for you, Talia, nor for my pack. Not anymore."

Tears welled up in my eyes and fell, but I continued to stare at him. He'd done it. My savior. He'd freed me from the tyranny of an unfair pack Alpha and a death decree hanging over my head.

I covered my mouth with my hand so that I didn't sob out loud. Instead, I swallowed hard. "Galen, I...."

He looked away. "It's okay."

"Thank you," I rushed to add, "I owe you my life."

He shook his head. "You don't owe me anything."

I put my hand on his arm and he groaned as though my touch hurt him. "Why won't you look at me?"

His jaw tightened, a muscle ticking just beneath his ear. Then he said through his teeth, "Because if I look at you, I might do something we'll both regret, and I don't want to do that. Not after everything you've been through."

A feeling flashed through me that I couldn't even begin to describe.

Hope? Fear? Or was this pure need?

I didn't know what it was, but I knew I needed to move closer. I pressed my hand against his back, then leaned forward so that I could touch my lips to his flesh, too. I kissed his skin, tasting the natural saltiness there.

He groaned and twisted around, sliding on top of me in one move and pushing me back into the mattress.

I welcomed the feel of his body heavy atop mine. Then I wrapped my legs around his waist, carefully trying to avoid his injuries, and pulled his face down to me for a kiss.

When our lips met, I gasped at the pleasure that shot through me. I wanted more. I arched up into his naked body, needing to get closer.

He moaned as I moved my fingers into his hair, holding him tight against me, his tongue sliding into my mouth.

I groaned at the pleasure arrowing deep into my core.

God, I wanted him. More than I'd ever wanted anyone.

With that thought, the pain of the past came crashing

down into me like an avalanche. My father's death. Maddox's rejection.

I couldn't do this. Not yet.

I stilled, and Galen clearly felt the change in me.

He pushed himself up on his hands and stared down at me. "Are you okay?"

I nodded, pressing my fingers to my mouth. I could still feel the imprint of his lips on mine, the scratch of his unshaven face on my cheek. I reached up and stroked the hair back from his forehead, but I didn't try to kiss him again.

He must have read something in my expression, because he gave a quirky little grin and shook his head slightly.

He was still on top of me, with barely a towel covering his body, and yet I could sense no aggression in him. No need to take or force me, even after the day he'd had. His natural state seemed to be more protector than aggressor, and I relaxed beneath him when I realized he had accepted my need to go slow.

He dropped his head and pressed his lips against mine, just holding there, like he was saying goodbye. Then he rolled to his side and stood up beside the bed, wincing.

"Sorry. I can't lie down on my side too long," he said. "My back's too sore."

I sat up and tucked my knees into my chest, embarrassed I'd pulled away from him barely one kiss into... whatever that might have developed into. "I'm sorry. I just..."

"It's totally fine." His tone was clipped. "I forgot that you're... untouched. I didn't mean to scare you."

I shook my head. "You didn't! You're... amazing. And I'm so grateful for what you did for me this morning."

His eyebrows drew together as he re-tied the towel around

his waist to cover himself. "I hope that's not why you let me kiss you. I don't need that sort of gratitude."

I hopped off the bed. "No, it wasn't like that. You're..."

I swallowed hard.

How did I say this without sounding ridiculous? "You're beautiful. Especially when you're... not dressed."

My face flamed, but it was worth the hideous feeling of embarrassment that shot through my whole body when he answered my stumbling explanation with a sudden grin.

"Yeah, well—" he began, but we were interrupted before he could go further.

"Galen!" a male voice called out from inside the house somewhere, sounding like one of his anxious Betas.

Galen's head whipped around. "That'll be Markus," he said, walking toward the door to my bedroom. "Thanks for patching me up, Talia."

"Of course," I whispered, as he walked out the door. Then I added, to myself, because he'd already left. "Thank you for saving my life, Galen. Again."

I sat down on the bed, wishing I could melt into a puddle and disappear. The truth was staring me in the face, and it was impossible to deny. I wanted Galen, the next Alpha to this pack.

CHAPTER 4
GALEN

I headed toward the front door, when Markus stood.

"Hey!" I called out to my Beta as I walked down the hall from the bedroom, my ankle feeling better with each passing minute. Talia must have done a good job of matching up the flesh with her stitching because the wound was already healing.

"You're back," he said, relief in his tone. "Thank God."

I grinned at him. "You didn't doubt me?"

His eyebrows drew together. "Of course not, but it still felt like an unnecessary move."

I shrugged. "I won, and demanded they leave Talia and our pack alone. They agreed. So hopefully the attacks will stop. For now, anyway."

I wasn't under any illusion that the peace I'd brokered with my blood this morning would last forever. Grudges this old and that ran so deep rarely disappeared overnight.

"Just give me a minute to get dressed and we can talk more

then," I told him, pointing at the door of the spare room I'd been using.

"Oh, that's what I came to tell you!" Markus said, slapping the side of his head like he'd forgotten something important. "There's absolute fucking chaos going on in town. I think we should get in there."

In town? What now?

"Okay, come with me and give me the run down," I said, indicating he should follow. I hurried into my room, threw my wet towel over a chair, and started grabbing my clothes. "What's going on?"

"I just got a call from Mikey, the guy who runs the liquor store. He said the witches are going insane. Blowing stuff up. Something's wrong, and I think the humans are gonna need our help."

"Shit..." I groaned, tugging on my boots, then cursed when the shoe hit my healing ankle. "What do you think it is?"

There was only one thing I knew that drove witches, as a group, insane like that. But I could be wrong. Hopefully I was.

Markus shook his head. "Not sure. I don't think I've ever seen anything like Mike was talking about."

I hadn't seen the madness in person, but my dad had told me the stories.

"I think I might know," I said grimly. "Let's go. I'm gonna grab Talia."

Markus frowned at me. "You're bringing her with you?"

"Of course." She was safest with me. "Let's go. Talia!"

She came running down the hall, her red and gold hair flying around her face. "Yeah?"

"We need to go into town, now. I'll explain on the way."

She nodded and followed us down the hall and out the front door.

I jumped in my truck. Markus sat in the passenger side and Talia hopped in the back, hovering in the gap between us.

When we were on the road, heading into town, Talia piped up. "So, what's happened? Why the rush?"

I glanced in the rear-view mirror, meeting her gaze. "I think the demons are infecting the witches."

"Demons? What do you mean?" she asked, a note of fear in her voice.

She was right to be concerned. Demons brought a whole other level of batshit crazy.

"Seriously?" Markus said. "How do you know that?"

"I've heard about it before," I told him, putting my foot down harder on the accelerator. "Demons affect all of us differently, but when a demon touches a witch, they go insane. They'll fight and scream and throw magic around the place. They're aggressive, too, according to the stories. I can't imagine what they'll be doing to the townsfolk."

I planted my foot even harder against the accelerator and the truck raced toward town. I wanted to be wrong, but since I'd seen that demon trying to seduce Talia out of the alleyway, I'd known they'd surface again.

That sighting hadn't been a chance encounter. It was the beginning of something big.

"Is it permanent?" Talia asked. "The changes to the witches?"

Good question.

"No, it's not. It only lasts a day or so. It's like an infection. It works through their system after a while, but they can do a lot of damage in that time."

More than I wanted to think about.

The town came up on the horizon and, even from this distance, smoke billowed up from the buildings.

"Oh, Jeezus. I hope we're not too late," I muttered.

I hit the outer edges of town and drove down the main street. Chaos and mess were everywhere. When a witch blasted a human man with magic, knocking him through a glass shop front, I slammed on the brakes. The truck fishtailed down the road and narrowly avoided a rabid group of howling witches that appeared seemingly out of nowhere.

"Holy shit," Markus said, while Talia's expression in the rear-view mirror was round-eyed with shock.

The car slid sideways and somehow landed right outside my bar and apartment with a loud screech.

I glanced at the building where everything seemed quiet and normal. *Thank fuck.*

"Talia, you get in there and stay safe. Markus and I need to help the humans."

Markus jumped out of the truck and we followed suit, Talia slamming the car door shut. It was an insane scene with black-robed women walking the streets flinging magic this way and that as if uncaring of any consequences.

People screamed, fire burst out of shops, and a huge crash sounded in the distance. That one sounded bad, like a big car crash.

"Fuck. I've gotta go check that out." Markus ground out between his teeth.

I grabbed hold of Markus's arm. He was already chomping at the bit to run after the berserker witches. "Be careful, and if you can help any humans without shifting, please do. They don't need to see wolf shifters on the same day they realize witches and magic are real."

Markus nodded and took off running down the road.

Talia looked at me, her jaw set. "I'm going to help."

"No. I want you safe."

"Then why did you bring me?"

I opened my mouth to respond then realized that she had a point. If I had really wanted her safe, then I should have left her at home with my dad. "You're right, but can you try and stay out of the witches' way? Try and help any humans get in their cars and leave rather than engaging with anyone non-human."

She nodded. "No problem."

We took off in opposite directions, and even though a part of me wanted to keep Talia by my side, we now had bigger issues to worry about than her stupid old pack.

As I rounded a corner, I came face to face with a witch whose hair frizzled out in every direction. She had a look of madness in her eyes.

She shot spears of magic straight at a hairdressing salon. I launched myself at her to push her off-balance. I didn't want to shift unless I had to, but when she lurched straight back onto her feet and swiveled to face me, a light of rage had joined the madness in her expression.

She threw back her head and cackled, and there was nothing human or rational about that sound whatsoever.

Uh oh.

There was no time to strip off and shift nicely. Instead, I leapt into my wolf form and stood on all paws before her, growling a warning.

She ignored me, throwing her arm forward and sending a blast of flame straight at my already-injured hip.

I ducked away with only a tiny puff of air between me and incineration.

I didn't want to hurt her, but she was leaving me no choice. I readied myself to launch. A small wolf landed on all four paws between us, growling and snarling at the witch.

Talia? Little Talia wanted to defend *me?*

A mixture of respect and fear rippled through me. If the witch got to her with one of those flames, she would be nothing but ash. A howl tore out of my throat... but then I quieted, shocked at what was happening.

The witch was staring at Talia and slowly backing away. Talia advanced, step by growling step.

It almost looked as if the witch was afraid of my little wolf defender, and that the fear had cut through some of the madness at last.

The witch released a strange shriek, and then turned and ran off down the street. I let her go. She no longer seemed inclined to shoot magic flame.

The small wolf in front of me stared after the witch. I came up beside her and nuzzled her shoulder in thanks. She cocked her head to the side, looking in the direction the witch had run, then shook her body in a violent manner, as if she'd experienced something distasteful.

Then she seemed to come back into herself. She touched her nose to mine, just for a moment, but the ripple that ran through me had nothing to do with fear, and everything to do with lust.

I needed to shift back to human, and fast, and finish the task at hand, before I lost concentration.

AFTER THAT CRAZY-HAIRED WITCH DISAPPEARED, something seemed to change in relation to the insanity going on around us. The tension lowered a notch, and at last, within only a few hours, all the witches responsible for the damage came to my bar to find me.

They were mostly back in their right minds, remorseful and worried about what this meant for their future in the town.

"Firstly, you need to go home. Heal yourselves," I told them. "But it may be best that you don't come into town for a while."

"Some of us weren't affected," a young blonde in the back of the group piped up. "Not many, but a few of us. What should *we* do?"

"You could focus on fixing the damage done in town, then, by those of you who were hurt by this event. Fix the broken windows and the shops. Do everything you can while the humans are hunkered down in their homes tonight, then you'll probably need to talk about getting some memory spells cast."

An older witch with bite marks on her face nodded. "I can start that process."

"Leave," I told them. "Those of you that are capable, fix the town. The rest of you, go home and rebuild your health and your strength."

The witches left en masse, most of them beaten and bruised, and all of them regretful. Many had been hurt by the wolves and others had injured themselves in their frenzy. Paramedic and police sirens sounded in the distance, likely coming to help the humans even though the danger seemed to have passed.

It was a mess. All of it.

I wanted them out of my bar and gone.

The next afternoon, I went back to town to check things out in the light of a fresh day. I stood outside the bakery and studied my surroundings. The witches had done a great job of putting the town to rights. Most of the shops looked the same as they always had, and the streets were clear of debris.

From the smiles on the faces of most humans walking past the bakery, the witches had thrown some memory spells around as well, because there wasn't a frown—or a police car, for that matter—anywhere to be seen.

I jumped out of the truck and walked over to my bar. I had to unpack a shipment of alcohol that had arrived that morning.

"Come on in," I called to Talia, who I'd brought with me. I still didn't want her out of my sight. I didn't trust anyone to be as vigilant as me, and after she'd saved my life yesterday, I owed her.

She sat at the bar while she waited for me to finish the work that needed to get done, drinking water and being altogether too patient. Anyone else would have been bored, or complaining, but not her.

It took me an hour to put everything where I wanted it. Talia offered to help, of course, but I figured it would take longer to explain where everything went than to do it myself, so I just got the task done.

I released a sigh and wiped the sweat off my brow as I finished the final box and returned to Talia. "Give me five minutes to call the bar manager, then we can go."

It was close to dinner and my stomach was grumbling.

Of course, that was when my front door opened.

"Galen?" The voice was female and one I didn't recognize.

I twisted around as a group of women walked into the bar. Four of them, with uncannily bright blue eyes harboring the light of magic that gave them away as witches.

Their spines were straight, their clothes dark, and there wasn't an injury among them. These four clearly weren't part of the coven that had created havoc yesterday.

"Yeah, that's me," I said, walking forward to confront them.

I wasn't worried about their intent because I had protective wards on the doors of this place. There was no way they would have gotten through those, if they'd meant me or my people any harm.

The group stopped in the middle of the bar.

One of the women stepped forward and lifted her chin. "We've come to ask for sanctuary."

I crossed my arms over my chest and stared down at her. "Come again?"

"We live a few towns over and heard about what happened here yesterday."

I nodded. "Yeah, it was a damn shame. The witches from our local coven have never caused the town any problems before."

In fact, I'd considered some of them friends, until yesterday. Today, I was a little more wary.

"We heard you were a kind man, with an even temper," the woman said. She had obviously been deemed spokesperson for the others.

I let my amusement show on my face. "You don't need to blow smoke up my ass. What do you want?"

The woman blinked like she didn't understand what I meant.

Then she inclined her head with a regal tilt. "We want sanctuary."

I let my arms fall to my sides with a casual air, but inside, I said to myself, *oh crap*. I plonked down on a bar stool next to Talia, giving myself a moment to process her request.

The head witch's gaze roamed over Talia as if she'd only just noticed her. She frowned a little before turning back to me. "Will you help us?"

"You're gonna have to be clear about what you actually need. I'm not a church." And I'd never offered sanctuary to anyone before, except Talia, and I'd kidnapped her first.

"No, but you're a strong Alpha with pack lands where we can hide."

My mouth dropped open. So, she wasn't kidding about the sanctuary.

"Why do you need to hide?"

All four of the witches rolled their eyes in unison. The one at the front took another small step forward. "You know there are demons around. We can't protect ourselves."

"And you think I can?"

What was I going to do that their magic couldn't?

The witch to the leader's left, sporting a head of curly red hair, stepped forward, her voice urgent. "Please. We can help your pack with whatever you need. Food growth, potions, healing. We just need somewhere safe to stay for a while. Please."

It was the second please that got me.

I rubbed my face, and then hauled myself to my feet. "Let me talk to my father, the real Alpha of our pack, and I'll let you know. Okay?"

The redhead looked like she was going to protest but the one at the front put a hand on her arm and shook her head.

Then she turned to me. "We'll come by tomorrow for your answer. Thank you for your time, Galen."

They left, just as mysteriously as they'd arrived.

I turned to Talia, who hadn't spoken a single word while they were here. "Any comments? You've been pretty quiet today."

She shrugged. "I have lots of comments, but it's your choice, Galen. You're the Alpha."

I ran a hand through my hair and collapsed back onto the

stool beside her. The funny thing was, I wasn't. My dad was still with us, so technically *he* was the Alpha of the pack, not me. I felt like a kid dressing up and pretending to be the leader. Nothing about this responsibility felt real, or normal.

"There is something I'd like to tell you," Talia whispered.

I narrowed my eyes at the paleness of her face. "Of course. Anything."

She glanced down at the floorboards and my heart ped up. Was it something to do with those witches that had just left? Or something new?

What was wrong now?

CHAPTER 5
TALIA

I blew out my breath. I didn't really want to have this conversation, but I needed to tell someone what had been eating at me since the witch attack yesterday. Galen seemed to be the most knowledgeable and trustworthy person around me.

"How much do you know about the demons?" I asked him.

Galen frowned. "I thought you wanted to tell me something? That's a question."

"It's sort of related," I admitted. "I want to talk about the demons, but I was wondering how much you know about them. You knew straight away that they were the reason the witches were going berserk yesterday, so... can you tell me what else you know about them?"

He sighed and leaned back against the bar, looking way too strong and sexy for my liking. Being around Galen made it hard to concentrate on anything else, sometimes.

"Well," he said slowly, "I only know what my father's told me."

"Which is…?"

He scratched his chest through his t-shirt with one hand and a strange quiver of heat rippled through my belly.

"That the presence of demons affects us all differently," he said.

"Us?" I asked, not understanding.

"Yeah, the paranormals. Apparently, wolves get more aggressive, more agitated. The witches become insane, like you saw last night. They don't seem to affect humans as much, but that's just a guess."

I nodded. "So, if they come near you or me, you think it'll make us more aggressive?"

He shrugged. "That's what Dad always said. But I don't think we start acting ferocious after just one encounter. I think they need to be around for a long time, or maybe they need to touch us. I'm not really sure."

Our gazes clashed.

"Why?" he asked.

I couldn't put it off any longer; I had to tell him. "Um… because I saw one yesterday."

Galen jerked, sitting up straight on his bar stool. "You did? Another one? When?"

"After you were attacked, and I saved you from that witch. As she ran off, I saw something move out of the corner of my eye. It was a demon. Another one." I dug my fingernails into my palms, enjoying the sting of the little bit of pain.

There was something about the demons that fascinated me. I knew I should fear them because they were bad. And on one level, I was scared. But I was also strangely intrigued by them.

When I saw one, I always felt the need to move closer, to

see if the fire they were made from burnt me, or whether it would totally consume me, if I touched one.

"Okay. What happened? Did it call to you again?" Galen's tone was demanding, suspicion etched into every line on his face. Was he suspicious of the demon presence? Or of me?

I nodded, unable to explain the pull properly. It hadn't been like last time, when I'd felt like I was in a trance and unable to control myself. This time, I'd been fully conscious, and yet I still wanted to move forward and be with the demon. See where it took me.

Galen groaned and shook his head, looking away.

I understood he was frustrated with me, and this whole situation. The demons were a new force and seemed to be wreaking havoc everywhere. The last thing he needed was some sort of beacon for the things, especially considering I currently lived in his unwell dad's house.

The silence dragged on, so finally I said, "Ah, is it okay if we run an errand on the way back to the pack?"

I needed a few things and since Galen didn't really like me being in town by myself, I needed to take this time to do a bit of shopping.

Galen glanced up. "What sort of errand?"

"I need to go to the drug store, and then a friend's house. I left my address book at her place, and I need to call my aunt. She'll probably be frantic by now."

I'd realized yesterday that I still hadn't called my mother's sister to tell her I was staying in town. I'd accidentally left my address book at Kylie's place.

Galen dragged himself to his feet. "I suppose. But I've gotta get back to Dad. Will it take long?"

I was about to tell him I'd be quick. The front door opened and two guys from the pack walked in.

"Hey Markus. Darius," Galen said, nodding toward the men.

"Hey." Markus nodded back. "You weren't answering your phone. Your dad wants you."

Galen groaned and walked around the bar, picking up his cell from where he'd stashed it.

"Shit. I think it's on silent." He grabbed his keys. "Come on. We've gotta go."

I jumped to my feet and pressed my hands together, palm to palm. "I really need to go to Kylie's, and the drug store. I'm sorry I didn't think to go earlier by myself."

Not that he would have let me go anywhere alone.

Galen ran a hand through his hair, a frown tugging at his brows. "My dad needs me."

"I can take her," Darius said. "Happy to help."

Galen stared at the new wolf. I glanced between all three of the guys in front of me. I wasn't totally comfortable with Darius, but I wasn't worried about him either.

He never looked at me inappropriately, but he was definitely interested in me for some reason. I wasn't sure if it was because of my relationship with Galen, or if there was something else.

"I'm okay with that, if you are," I said, addressing Galen.

He glanced at his cell, probably balancing out the time it would take to do what I needed to do, versus getting back to the pack.

"That would be great, actually," he said, then glanced at Markus. "You coming with me?"

Markus looked at me, then Darius. "Nah, I'll ride with them. All my shit's in my car anyway. You go. Your dad needs you."

Galen looked at me, raising his eyebrows as he asked, "You sure?"

I nodded, my heart tugging in my chest at his show of concern. "Yeah. Absolutely. I'll only be an hour or so. See you back at the pack then."

Galen nodded and left, and I was alone with the two other wolf shifters.

Darius, who'd been smiling a minute ago, was now frowning heavily, lines creasing in his brow.

"You didn't need to stay with me," he said to Markus. "I can drive your truck fine."

"I don't think so," Markus said with a grin.

I grabbed my bag and headed out the door. The sun was slowly dropping out of the sky, but it was still light enough for the shops to be open a little longer.

"Thanks for doing this," I told Darius as we waited for Markus, who took a little longer to head out the door.

"No problem," Darius said, looking annoyed, his lips pulled tight and down.

It seemed like Darius was pretty pissed off that Markus was coming with us. I had no idea why. I was only doing a shopping errand and I thought it was pretty clear to the whole pack that I was Galen's to protect.

I wasn't available to any other wolf.

We jumped in the truck and drove straight over to Kylie's house. She was home, luckily, and gave me my book that I'd left there.

I didn't stop to explain what was going on, just thanked her, reassured her I was okay, and ran back to the car.

"Where to next?" Markus asked from the front seat.

"Ah, the drug store please," I said.

Markus drove me to the only drug store in town, humming

away as he drove while Darius glared out the window the whole time.

He was definitely annoyed. Had he wanted me to himself? Why would he? Didn't he know that Galen would hurt him if Darius did something to me, or tried anything romantically?

When Markus pulled up outside the shop, I jumped out. "Thanks. I'll only be a minute."

I walked inside, glancing around. I needed the women's section, for my monthly which was due. Which aisle were the tampons in? I turned to the left, set on quickly hunting down what I needed, and almost ran into Samantha, a friend from my old pack.

Happiness flooded me. We'd grown up together and her family had lived only a few houses down from mine. "Sam! I…"

Sam's eyes widened when she saw me, then a dirty look crossed her face like she'd sucked on a lemon. She lifted her pointed chin in the air and turned her head away. "Don't talk to me."

I stared at her, shocked to my core.

"Oh, ah…"

What could I say? That, in that moment when I'd seen my friend, I'd forgotten my old pack hated my guts? That they'd been told to kill me on sight?

"Sorry."

As I turned away; Sam grabbed her cell phone out of her bag and began to text frantically.

Panic hit me in the chest with the weight of a fist. She could be calling for help, or she could be just bitching to someone back at the pack. Either way, I needed to hurry.

I raced away from her, looking for the aisle I needed. There. I snatched up the few products I needed for my week ahead and ran to the counter to pay.

Three people stood in line in front of me, and I clung to the small boxes in my hand. I couldn't afford to stand here forever. Should I just drop them and leave?

One person finished their purchase and walked away, then there were only two people in front of me.

I tapped my foot, a shriek rising in my throat. Sam seemed to have disappeared, but the panic in my heart hadn't. Should I cut and run?

I glanced out the window beside the counter. Darius and Markus were out the front, sitting in the car and both looking bored. There wasn't any danger. It was all in my head.

There wasn't anyone coming for me. I had to calm down.

Only one person in front of me now.

Breathe. Just breathe.

Galen had brokered a deal for my freedom, hadn't he? He'd told me I was safe. I had to remember that.

Memories of last night came flooding back, including the kiss we'd shared. It had been, by far, the hottest kiss I'd ever had.

In the past, I'd often wondered about sex, and how on earth it could feel natural to have a man put his dick inside my body. The very act sounded freaky and weird, and although I'd had confidence that with Maddox it would be okay, the idea of it had never seemed natural to me. Not at all.

But being with Galen yesterday had been totally different. I'd finally understood how sex could be simple and, dare I even think it, natural.

It would have been too easy to open my legs for him. Way too easy. In fact, every part of me had wanted my clothes to melt away so I could feel his hot, naked body against mine.

He would have whipped his towel away and kissed me, surged into me...

I shook my head, heat flooding my cheeks at the thoughts crowding my mind. Galen was dangerous for me. He made me feel different. Unlike me. He made me want to do things I've never done before.

The next person ahead of me was done, and it was my turn.

The salesgirl called me forward and I paid for my things, then headed outside. The sun was shining, and I was heading back to the pack for dinner. Everything was going to be okay.

I stopped dead in my tracks. Four men ran toward me down the street, all of them ex-pack members.

"Shit!" I raced for the car, yanked open the door, and jumped into the back seat. "Go! Those guys are coming for me."

Markus switched on the engine and threw the car into gear just as a fist bashed against my window.

"Get out of the car! Traitor!" Anthony yelled at me through the window.

I screamed, terrified he would break the glass with his next punch. "I thought Galen made a deal with you!"

"Fuck Galen!" Anthony yelled, his eyes showing a devilish hint of red.

Oh, no. Not the demons again.

What had Galen said? Demons made wolves extra-aggressive.

"Hold on!" Markus called as he hit the gas and we jumped into traffic, swerving to miss a car, then we zoomed out of town.

I put on my seat belt with trembling hands, then twisted around in my seat to see the four guys still running after our car.

"Whoa, that's insane," I whispered at the sight of them pumping their arms and legs and trying to catch us.

"They better not shift," Markus said, changing gears and

pushing the car even faster. "First the witches, now that bloody pack. Did you see his eyes?"

I settled into my seat, relaxing now that we were further away from town. "I thought I was seeing things."

Markus shook his head. "Not if you saw that red glimmer. Bloody demons."

He growled.

My gaze strayed to Darius who stayed remarkably silent. Didn't he have an opinion on the presence of demons? Or the fact that my old pack had just tried to grab me again, despite the deal Galen had supposedly struck with them?

But he didn't say a thing.

We were only a couple of minutes from the edge of pack territory. A woman darted out on to the road in front of the truck, waving her arms.

Markus yelled out, "Holy shit! Hold on."

He slammed on the brakes, the car fishtailing and skidding on the road.

I grabbed for the safety handle and clung tight, thankful I'd put on my seat belt when we left town.

I jerked forward, then slammed back as the car came to a stop.

"Stupid bitch. What is she doing?" Markus huffed as he opened the door and jumped out.

I followed, scrabbling to grab the handle and get out without my legs collapsing under me from nerves. I wanted to know what on earth this was about.

The woman knelt on the road, her knees in the dirt. She wore patched, colorful clothing which only the witches around us wore, but from which coven she belonged, I didn't know.

"Please," she begged. "You need to help me. Take me with you."

Her face was tear-streaked, and blackened ash touches were evident on her clothes, like she'd been burned. Or gotten too close to a fire.

"Are you okay?" I asked, unable to stay quiet while the Betas simply stood there, gaping at her.

"No. I'm not. Please. We need help. The demons are everywhere. My coven members are... hurt. They need help."

"No way." Markus shook his head. "We need to look after our own pack. And you need to go home."

"No, please..." She sobbed again, and my heart wrenched in my chest. We should help her. She didn't appear to be a threat to us.

Markus took my arm and pulled me back toward the car. "Come on, Talia. We need to get back. It's not safe here."

"But..." I stopped. I knew he was referring to my old pack members, who even now might have shifted and be racing after us. It was unfortunate for this poor woman, because if it wasn't for the fact that my pack were still hunting me, I would have stayed and fought for her right to be heard.

But Markus was correct: we needed to leave, and fast.

"Okay."

I'm sorry, I mouthed at the woman. She bowed her head and sobbed some more.

We climbed back into the truck and drove around the witch who was still kneeling on the ground.

I stared out the back window and watched her figure get smaller and smaller in the distance. My head spun with questions.

Was she part of the coven that had attacked the town yesterday? Maybe... but that didn't feel right.

Or was she part of the coven who'd come to ask Galen for sanctuary today?

I glanced to the front seat where Darius and Markus were sitting in silence. *Shit.* Should I say something to them about the witches who'd come to speak to Galen? Was it my place?

Probably not.

When we got back to the pack, Markus dropped me off at the Alpha's house and I bolted inside. Galen was nowhere to be seen.

"Talia, is that you?" the Alpha called out from his bed.

"It's me!" I stashed my products in my room then ran to him. "Hello, Alpha. Are you okay?"

He was sitting up in bed, but his skin was pale and he had dark smudges under his eyes. "Yes, I'm all right. Is Galen back yet?"

My heart thumped. Galen wasn't back? I walked up to his bedside. "Didn't he come and see you earlier?"

"Yes, but only for a moment. Then he sensed something outside, shifted, and took off. I'm not sure what he sensed, but he hasn't returned."

Fear tugged at my heart. Had it been another of my ex-pack members come to get me? Or something more dangerous?

I picked up the empty jug of water next to his bed and said, "I'll let you know when he gets back. I'll get you some fresh water now, then go wait for Galen. Is there anything else you need?"

He stared at me with his assessing gaze, then shook his head. "No. I'm fine. Thank you."

I hurried to the kitchen, filled up the jug for him, then returned it to the spot next to his bed. Job done, I then ran to the front door, where I sat down on the stoop and waited for Galen to return.

I had a lot to tell him. And a lot of questions to ask.

CHAPTER 6
GALEN

I was talking to Dad when I sensed the demon. Even though I shifted and took off, chasing down the scent, I never found the creature that had dared to come onto my pack lands. I followed the trail all the way to our border to the east, but I didn't go any further.

With everything that had been happening lately, with the witches and also with Talia, it wasn't worth being away too long. So, I turned around and headed home again.

I wanted to check on Dad and see if Talia was back yet. Stupid demons were making everything worse. We already had the issue of the pack wars, but add in crazy witches and demons trying to attract Talia for reasons I couldn't fathom, and my temper was bubbling through the roof.

I wanted to rip those demons apart.

I slowed my gallop once I neared home. Some of my people turned to me, smiling and waving as I trotted past. They probably assumed I'd just wanted to let off some steam with a run.

I needed a shower and something to eat.

I needed a woman too, but that wasn't happening anytime soon.

In fact, I didn't remember the last time I'd sated those urges within myself. Too long.

Talia was sitting on the front doorstep as she often did, waiting for me.

I shifted back to my human state as I reached the foot of the stairs. My heart pounded in my chest, not from the run or from the remnants of anger still pulsing through me, but from the desire I felt for her, and the lust mirrored in her eyes when she stared with a hungry look back at my naked body.

I lifted my chin, daring her without words to look her fill. As a wolf shifter, I was comfortable with my body and used to being naked around my pack. Talia should have been too, being a shifter herself. But there was a naïveté to her manner that was unusual in our pack.

Talia didn't look at me like she'd seen a hundred men naked before. With her, it was totally different. She made me feel something I'd never felt. Not even with Jessie.

I clenched my jaw at the single thought about my old girlfriend and forced my body not to react to Talia the way it wanted to.

Too late.

Heat and blood pulsed through me. There was no stopping the way my cock swelled in reaction to her.

I pretended to ignore my hard-on and jogged up the steps to push past her. "I need a shower. Give me five minutes and I'll be out to talk."

I rushed down the hall and shut the bathroom door behind me. I glared down at my swollen cock and growled. "You need to get your mind out of the gutter and on to the problem."

Cold water blasted out of the shower head and doused my overheated body.

I scrubbed my skin with the washcloth and soap. When I couldn't take the needling coldness any longer, I got out of the shower, dried myself, and put on a clean pair of jeans, sneakers, and a t-shirt.

When I finally felt a little more in control, of both my wolf and my human side, I walked into the kitchen where Talia was waiting with a plate of toasted sandwiches.

"I thought you might be hungry." She pushed the plate forward.

My stomach growled. Hell yes, I was hungry. I'd totally forgotten about dinner after the incident with the demon.

"Thanks." I sat down on the kitchen stool with relief, loving the way the yellow cheese oozed out onto the plate between the nicely toasted pieces of buttered bread.

I picked up the sandwich on the top of the pile and bit into it. I moaned as the greasy meal satisfied at least one kind of hunger that had been building inside of me.

I ate one, then the next, then set about devouring a third. When I finally finished, and licked my fingers clean, Talia came around and sat on the stool next to me.

"Your dad said you sensed something and went out to look for it?"

Her tone was questioning, politely asking for an answer.

"It was a demon," I said. "I scented it hanging around here. Which I don't really understand as we've never had a demon on our pack land before. At least, not to my knowledge."

I reached for the glass of water Talia put in front of me. "But with all the trouble they're causing at the moment, I guess I shouldn't be surprised. I mean, why stop with the witches?"

"I agree. I don't think they've stopped with just tormenting the witches."

My brows rose and I turned on the stool so I could face her properly. "What do you mean?"

"Well, some of my old pack members tried to attack me at the drug store earlier."

A growl rolled through my chest. After everything I had done to ensure at least a few years of peace? *Those assholes.*

"They fucking *what*? Are you okay?"

She nodded. "Yeah, I'm fine. Markus did a good job of driving the getaway car."

My gaze flew over her pale face, her thin neck, all the way to her hands. She seemed untouched but even so, anger swelled inside of me.

"Those bastards. We made a deal. I beat their Alpha. I let him live. They never should have been anywhere near you."

What was I going to do about this now? I'd tried everything I knew to keep Talia safe, and now the packs were going to be at war. Again.

I should have killed that bastard Alpha of theirs.

I looked at Talia and reached for her, unable to keep my hands to myself. I cupped her cheek and stared at her beautiful face, those dark eyes staring up at me with all the trust I could ever hope for in a woman.

"I'm so sorry," I said. "I never should have left you alone."

"I wasn't alone. I was with Markus and Darius. And it wasn't your fault." She narrowed her eyes at me. "You've done more for me than anyone has ever done, and I don't think it's entirely Maddox's pack's fault either."

I dropped my hand away from her face. "What do you mean?"

"They had a red glow in their eyes..."

I cursed again. "That does sound like a demon's touch."

"Exactly. But why? What do they want?" Talia asked. "And why now?"

I shook my head, unable to answer. I crossed my arms over my chest and grunted. I had no idea what the demons wanted, but I didn't want to stick around and just wait to find out.

"There's one other thing you should know." Talia bit her lip.

I narrowed my eyes at her. "Yeah? Tell me."

"We met a witch on the road. Actually, we almost ran her over."

"You what?"

Since when did witches lie down in the middle of our roads? They knew where all the pack borders were and mostly stayed clear of us.

"She begged us for help. Wanted us to take her home with us." Talia swallowed hard, her throat working with emotion. "I wanted to help her, but... I'm really worried about the witches, Galen. They're not safe. We need to help."

I groaned and thrust my fingers through my hair, pushing the wetness left over from the shower out of my eyes. "Talia, you know that's not a good idea."

"Then why didn't you tell those witches today that you couldn't take them in?"

I looked away, slightly annoyed at the reminder, and the knowledge that she could read me so well. "Because you never say no to a witch, not directly, and not without thinking about it first."

"That's not the reason," she said quietly.

I sighed. "You're right. I don't want to say no to them. I want to help. Just like you do. But my pack is not going to like it. Especially not after what happened in town yesterday."

The fight with the witches had left several of our pack wolves hurt, and most of them angry and wanting revenge.

"The witch today was from a different coven. I'm sure of it," she insisted. "And you're the Alpha while your father is unwell, Galen. You get to decide. Make the others understand."

I stared at her, loving the sudden fierceness in her face. "Why do you want to help the witches so much, Talia? You don't owe them anything. In fact, you took part in the fight yesterday to protect the humans. And me."

I still couldn't believe she'd stepped in to save me from that crazy witch. Sweet Talia. She looked so soft and fragile, beautiful like a rose. But she had a keen mind, and from what I'd now seen, the inner strength to step in and fight when she was needed. A courageous heart was a great asset in a pack member, and mate.

"We're all in the same boat," she said. "All fighting against the demons, and those witches need our help. I can't imagine turning away someone who truly needed help when I might be in a position to offer it."

I groaned as I stood up off my seat, then stretched my back. "I need to call a pack meeting. See what everyone has to say, because despite the pack hierarchy, and my ability to make decisions on behalf of them all, I still want to hear what everyone thinks."

Talia grinned as she got to her feet and stood before me. "Sounds like a great plan. Should we go now?"

I nodded. "Why not?"

A lot of the women would be putting their kids to bed, but I could rally up my Betas and get at least some others from the pack to attend.

I stuck my head in to check on my dad, who was sleeping soundly, then rallied the troops. Within five minutes, I was standing on the small stage at one end of the town hall, surrounded by five of my men, and looking out on the rest of our pack as members trailed in. It wasn't everyone, but there were enough here that I could get a sense of where people's heads were at.

When everyone was seated, I held up my hand to quiet the buzz, then began to speak.

My first announcement was met with surprise, and then anger. "A coven of witches approached me in the bar today, and I'm considering offering them the refuge they asked for.

"You wanna do... *what?*" Markus asked, his mouth tight and anger flaring in his eyes.

I crossed my arms over my chest, looking down at the other pack members. The same disbelief and anger filled their gazes.

Talia sat in the front row of seats and the heat of her gaze warmed my face.

"You heard me."

"But... why would we do that?" David asked.

I sighed. Why did I need to explain this to them? Couldn't they see that we were in a war?

"Because we need allies in this. There's a war on, whether you want to admit it or not. The demons are here for a reason, and I don't think it's just to cause havoc. They want something. So, until we work out what they're here for, we need to be in as strong a position as possible."

"Aligning with the witches won't make you stronger," Darius said, crossing his arms across his chest. "Look what happened yesterday."

I frowned at the man who'd been an outsider only a week ago. "The witches have powers we don't have. And they've always been good to have on side. I use them to keep my bar safe, and they put up wards around the cabin that kept Talia locked up as well."

All eyes slid to Talia sitting in the front row of seats.

I didn't look at her to see how she was handling their stares. Her face was probably as red as her hair.

Instead, I drew everyone's attention back to me. "Listen, guys. We need to work together on this."

"We?" Darius demanded. "Who's we?"

"My pack," I said, glaring at him, before looking at all the pack members who'd assembled in the hall.

They were observing my discussion with my Betas with interest, and from the collective look of trust in their eyes, would abide by any decision I deemed the right one.

"We need to consider this option, then *I* need to decide what's best for the group as a whole."

"No disrespect, Galen, but you know this is all Talia's fault," Tommy said, gesturing to her.

My eyebrows flew up. "Excuse me?"

"He's right," Theo said. "None of this would have happened if you'd let Talia go. Instead, you grabbed her, and kept her, even when it was obvious she was going to be more trouble than she was worth."

Never. I'd never say that.

"None of this is her fault." I growled at my guys. "Not the fact that her old pack kicked her out, or the demons causing havoc in town. These are separate issues."

"Galen, he has a point," Markus said quietly.

"You're wrong," Theo said, glaring at me.

They weren't going to stop and the anger in me was building. They were wrong about Talia and pointing their fingers at the victim in all this was making me even madder.

"No!" I all but roared at them. "Talia is not up for discussion here. She is my responsibility and all of you will keep your goddamn mouths shut."

The guys took a step back. Talia's hand crept up to her throat as she stared at me.

I panted hard, my breath heaving in and out of my chest.

"Enough." I growled again. "Now, I don't know how many families, children, or women are in this witch coven, but if I offer them sanctuary, and I said *if*, they will need housing, land, and food."

Theo groaned. "Fuck. We don't exactly have a lot of extra anything, Galen."

"I know. But we have land, and they have magic. So let's see what they offer when I speak to them again, okay?"

The guys grumbled around me, and I tried to calm my wolf down. I didn't mind the fact that my guys didn't agree with me. In fact, I welcomed the challenge. But throwing their hatred at Talia while we were discussing the witches wasn't fair.

"Talia and I will go back to the bar tomorrow, and I'll talk to the coven some more. But just in case I decide to offer them sanctuary, and that's a big *if*, I know how you all feel and will take it on board."

They all nodded, seemingly okay with my response.

I continued. "But I need more information from our pack too. So can you guys, Markus and David, go and speak with any of the other bachelors, see if they have spare rooms, see if you can shuffle some of the people around to make some space?"

Markus groaned. "Okay. Will do."

I glanced at my watch. It was dark now. Time for bed.

"Everyone." I addressed the group as a whole. "Head home. I'll run the perimeter tonight. You all get some sleep."

As the crowd filed out, Talia's voice piped up.

"You can't do that all night," she said, her first words since stepping into the meeting hall. "You're still injured."

I wanted to roll my eyes. "I'm fine."

I hadn't had a woman looking over me for years, and it felt... strange. But not unwelcome.

"She's right," David said. "I saw you limping home after your fight with the Northwood pack. You all right?"

All eyes turned to me with a more critical air.

I put up my hands. "I'm fine. A few scratches, but Talia sewed up my leg and my back will heal. No problem."

"I'll do the first half of the night, if someone can cover me after three a.m.," David said, ignoring me and glancing around the remaining group.

Theo put up his hand. "Me and Billy will take over at three. Have you got someone to double up with you?"

David nodded. "My brother will run with me."

I risked a glance at Talia, pride blossoming in my chest at the way my Betas rallied to support not only me, but each other.

"Thanks, guys."

I took Talia's elbow and we walked home. Together.

CHAPTER 7
TALIA

I was shivering, and I couldn't stop. Galen and I had walked back to the Alpha's house, and he was setting up to sleep on the couch while I was sitting on my bed shaking like a leaf.

I glanced toward the ensuite bathroom. Maybe a hot shower would help?

I pushed myself to my feet and moved into the tiled room. I flicked on the water, my teeth chattering so hard they were clacking in my mouth.

Steam began to rise, fogging up the mirror. I was freezing, damn it. What was wrong with me? I pulled off my clothes and dropped them to the floor, and hopped under the water.

"Ahh…"

Heat enfolded me, beating down on my shoulders and back. I shivered again, but when I turned and let the hot water flow over my face and down my chest, the shaking finally began to subside.

Why had the Betas all blamed me for the recent stuff that

had happened to them? I hadn't caused the initial attack to the pack, or my father's death, or Galen kidnapping me, either.

I'd been playing with the cards I'd been dealt the best I could but feeling their anger toward me was... hard.

I hadn't wanted any of this to happen and if my world hadn't been horrifically turned upside down, I would be married to Maddox now, living in the small house he'd built for us and dreaming of a future filled with children.

I would never have met Galen.

Sadness tugged at me at the thought, the feeling dragging me down, closer to the darkness of despair. I'd done a good job recently of pushing away the emotions that surrounded me about my father's murder, and my mate's rejection.

But now, I couldn't seem to stop the sudden need to lie down and not get up again.

I turned off the water, dried myself quickly, then staggered back to the bed. I managed to pull on some panties and a tank top to sleep in before there was a knock at my door.

"Talia?" Galen called through the closed door.

"Yeah?" My pillows were so close. I needed to just climb in between the covers, and then I could finally sleep.

What a day.

"Can I come in?"

I sighed. It was his room, and his house. What was I going to say? No?

"Okay."

The door opened and Galen snuck in quietly, then shut the door behind him.

He was wearing a loose pair of running pants and a cut away black tank that showed every inch of his muscled arms. "I wanted to check on you and see if you were okay."

I nodded at him from where I sat on the bed. "I'm fine."

"You don't look fine. You look upset, actually."

I shrugged and stared at the carpet before me, feeling numb. "I just wanna go to sleep."

Galen walked closer, then sat on the bed next to me. "I'm here if you wanna talk."

I closed my eyes, afraid I'd cry again. The man next to me had seen enough of my tears for a lifetime. "I don't. I just need sleep."

Galen stood and moved to the top of the bed. "Okay, then. Climb in."

He held back the blankets for me. I didn't stop to think about how sweet and caring the gesture was; I simply crawled up the mattress and slid between the covers.

When I lay my head on the pillow and closed my eyes, I could still feel his presence in the room.

I glanced up and saw him staring down at me. "Are you going to stay?"

He shook his head, but then knelt down beside the bed and used a gentle touch to push the hair off my forehead and stroke my head. "None of this is your fault, Talia."

I sniffed, still intent on never crying in front of Galen again. "I know."

"No matter what anyone says. My pack, yours. Maddox, or the Alpha. None of them are right. You're a victim in all of this."

My heart ached to hear him say everything I needed to hear. To know that he understood how I felt made all the difference.

"Thank you," I managed to whisper, before I shut my eyes again.

I couldn't do any more tonight. It had been such an intense day. Between Galen's fight this morning, to the meeting tonight, I felt stretched too thin. Hollow in places I'd once been full.

Galen pressed his lips to my temple and said, "If you need me, I'm only a room away. Okay?"

I nodded, and he quietly left.

That night I dreamt about being pregnant, though I never saw the baby, nor the man who'd given it to me.

I knew it wasn't Maddox's. Somehow, I knew it was Galen's.

Galen

The next morning, I got up early, grabbed a banana, and went out to meet my guys who'd been on guard duty all night. I needed a distraction, and preferably some good news.

I still didn't know what I was going to do about the witches who'd asked to move onto pack land. My job as acting Alpha in my father's stead was to keep my pack safe, but if I chose to take in the witches, I could be putting everyone in danger—witches and shifters alike.

Darius was against it; that was obvious. And so were most of my Betas and other pack members. Not Talia. She thought as I did—that the witches needed our help, and we should give it if we could.

For me, witches had always been great allies in a fight. They could be valuable when it came to the final fight, which there always was in wars like this.

The witches had already shown their weakness to the demons' influence, but that didn't mean they couldn't help to strengthen our numbers.

I still needed to think about it.

Once I'd checked in with my guys and learned nothing had come up overnight that worried me, I went home.

Talia seemed to still be asleep, her door shut, which was unusual for her. She was generally up at the crack of dawn, but yesterday seemed to have broken her somewhat. We all had our limits and she'd gone through a lot lately.

So, instead of checking on her, I snuck into my dad's room, where he was already sitting up and drinking water.

"Morning, Dad."

"Hey, son. How are you this morning?"

He was pale, and looked thinner than he had yesterday, but his mood was happy.

I smiled as I sat down on the chair next to his bed. "Needing some of your advice, if that's okay?"

"Always," Dad said, shifting on the bed so that he could sit higher. "What's wrong?"

I leaned back in the chair and sighed. "It's the witches."

"What about them?"

"Did Talia, or anyone else, tell you about what happened in town the other day?"

Dad nodded. "Tony came by and gave me a run down."

Tony was Markus's father, and one of my dad's oldest friends.

"Well, yesterday, another coven came by the bar and asked me if I'd let them move on to our pack grounds."

My dad's eyebrows rose high on his forehead, but he didn't say anything, so I continued.

"Sanctuary, they called it." I huffed out a laugh. "I don't know what to do. The demons are a real threat to the witches, and our pack. So, would I be endangering our people if I moved them in, or would their magic give us protection? I'm not sure which way to go."

Or what was going to be needed in what I felt was an inevitable fight.

Dad leaned back against his pillows. "What do you want to do?"

That was an easy answer. "Me? I want to help them."

They needed my help, and I'd always struggled to turn anyone away who was actually in need.

The strong were there to help the weak; that was the purpose of men like me.

"Then perhaps that is the answer," my father said.

I groaned. "That's not giving me advice, Dad. The pack doesn't want the witches here. In fact, some of my Betas are blaming Talia for everything bad that's happened. It's a mess."

My dad grinned, his bright white teeth flashing in the dim light of the room. "You're a good man, Galen. You're a great leader for our people."

My heart squeezed hard in my chest. I wasn't ready to lose my dad, not yet. "Tell me what to do, Dad. You're still our Alpha."

"Do what your gut tells you to do," he said. "Even if it means going against your pack, or your Betas. You're the Alpha for a reason, and your instincts won't let you down."

I clenched my jaw a little too tight, then asked, "What about Talia?"

"What about her?"

"Should I let her go? Drive her to the border and let her get to safety?"

The very idea of never seeing her again hurt on a level I didn't want to admit.

Dad shook his head. "No. It's way past that point now. You need to keep her safe, and safe for Talia at the moment is with you."

Relief winged through my chest at his words. I'd hoped that was the case, but even I knew I was blinded by my feelings for her. "You think so?"

My dad nodded. "I do. I know you've been alone since Jessie passed..."

"Dad..."

"We never really talked about it, Galen, but..."

I got to my feet. I didn't want to discuss what had happened to the woman I'd loved. "It's okay, Dad. It was a long time ago."

"Galen."

I walked to the door and opened it. "Thanks for the chat, Dad."

An awkward silence stretched between us.

Talia's bedroom door opened, and she walked out into the hallway, fully dressed in jeans and a yellow t-shirt the color of sunshine. "Morning."

My heart did a little dance at the sight of her face. "Good morning. How'd you sleep?"

"Like the dead," she said with a smile, slipping past me and walking into Dad's room. "Good morning, Alpha. Can I make you some eggs for breakfast?"

Dad perked up, the light of happiness flickering in his eyes.

"Yes, please."

"Scrambled?" She walked over to his windows and opened the curtains.

"Yes. Just two."

"I know, Alpha." Talia smiled, then walked over to me. "Would you like some breakfast, as well?"

I nodded, enjoying the fact that she was looking after my father so well, even though my wolf was a touch jealous at being second priority in her mind. "Please."

Talia headed to the kitchen, and I watched her leave.

I was already protecting Talia from the very real threat of her old pack, and the demons that seemed more than a little interested in her. Could I afford to split our defences and take in the witches as well? My heart said yes, though the worry that came with it was a heavy burden.

I nodded at my dad as a way of saying thanks and goodbye, then followed Talia into the kitchen. "After breakfast, we'll head into town and speak to the witches, okay?"

Talia lifted her gaze from the egg cracking she'd been doing and met my gaze. "Okay."

She stared at me, as though she was considering her next words, but then she bent her head to the task and continued making breakfast.

I took five minutes to have a quick shower, check on my injuries that were healing nicely, and dress into a shirt and a pair of jeans.

I had a meeting with a coven, after all.

Thanks to Talia, we ate a hearty breakfast before driving into town.

"Do you know what you're going to tell them?" she asked, when we were about halfway to the bar.

"Yeah, I do."

"Good," Talia said with a nod and a smile, and I couldn't help but laugh.

Did she read minds, too?

CHAPTER 8
TALIA

I'd just gotten around to pouring some waters for Galen and myself when the witches burst in the front door of the bar as if they couldn't contain their eagerness.

There were more of them today—by my count about nine of them—but the same woman with long dark hair was at their lead.

"Good day." She bowed her head at Galen, her expression grave.

The redhead from yesterday stared at me, and I wasn't sure why. She was assessing me intently, that was for sure. And she didn't seem happy with what she found in her assessment, either, though I couldn't pinpoint how I knew that. Maybe a slight tightening of the skin around her eyes and the way her lips pursed as she finally turned away.

Did she want Galen for herself or one of her friends? Was she thinking I was a threat to him partnering up with one of the witches? Because I wasn't. Sure, we'd kissed a little, but nothing was certain between us.

"Hello. I didn't get your names yesterday." Galen stepped close to the leader, gesturing for the group to come further in and take a seat wherever they could.

The dark-haired leader pointed to her chest. "I'm Marguerite, and this is Telly." She indicated the redhead, standing to her left. "And Sarah." She pointed to her right.

My gaze was drawn to Sarah. She had long blonde hair and bright blue eyes. She looked about my age, and seemed as terrified as I'd likely feel, walking into an Alpha's place of business and demanding refuge.

"You all know me. I'm Galen. This is Talia." He indicated me, but the witches barely spared me a glance. Except the redhead, who looked in an uncomfortably intense way.

"Have you decided on our fate?" Marguerite asked.

I wanted to roll my eyes at the dramatic words, but declined the childish move. Giving him the weight of their coven's 'fate' seemed a little heavy to me. It wasn't up to Galen to save them, or protect them if he didn't want to, for that matter.

"Yes," Galen answered calmly. He was more mature than me, clearly. "You are all free to come and stay on my pack lands. I will grant you sanctuary while the demons are still a threat to us all."

Relief rippled through the room.

"Thank you," Marguerite said, holding her hands together in a prayer-type of position and bowing her head over her fingers.

"We do have to discuss the particulars, of course. Timing, and how many of you there are. What we do about housing, food, that kind of thing," Galen added.

Marguerite exchanged glances with Telly, to her left, before answering. "There are only the nine of us. We are a small coven.

All unmarried. No children. The witches you see here are our whole group."

Galen glanced back at me, and I nodded, but didn't speak. That certainly made it easier on the pack, assuming these women would all pitch in and help.

He crossed his arms over his chest. "When do you want to move in?"

Marguerite smiled, the first time I'd seen that look on her face, and it transformed her from serious to attractive. She looked much younger when she smiled. "Would now be too soon?"

Galen laughed and the sound ricocheted around the room. The tension in the air began to dissipate as the witches responded to his friendly signals.

"Well, yes. Give my pack and me a few hours to get the place ready for your arrival. But if you'd like to meet at the territory border around seven this evening, we'll escort you in and arrange everything then."

Marguerite inclined her head, serious once again and as regal as a queen. "Thank you, Alpha. We will all see you at seven."

The nine of them swept out of the room in a flurry of black clothes and flowing hair.

I exhaled the breath I hadn't realized I'd been holding. "Why do I feel like they're gonna be trouble?"

Galen twirled to look at me, his eyebrows shooting sky high. "Don't say that. You were totally *for* the plan to move them in. I can't have you changing your mind now."

The vehemence in his tone surprised me. Why would my single opinion sway a man like him?

I slid off the bar stool where I had been perched with my glass of water. "Oh, I haven't changed my mind. It's just that nine women who don't usually share their space with men, or children, or... anyone non-magical, are about to move in with the pack. They might cause a little more trouble than I first thought."

I chewed on my lip, worrying the flesh. "But I still think you're doing the right thing bringing them in."

Galen nodded, though his brow was furrowed.

"What's wrong?" I asked, though I was pretty sure I knew what was worrying him. "It's a lot, isn't it? You're protecting me, your pack, and now a whole coven of witches. Female witches who you didn't even know at all before yesterday."

He stared at me, his eyes wide and his wolf burning deep within.

I took a couple of steps closer to him. "You're not even Alpha yet, and you're doing fantastic things, Galen. For your own people, for others, and for me."

I was within touching distance of him now and couldn't stop the desire to reach out and close the gap.

So I did. I took his fingers in mine, tangling them together so that it felt as if our pulses beat as one. I stood like that for a long moment, staring at the ground and loving the feel of his skin against mine. His pulse raced in tandem with mine. Then he tugged me closer still, and I pressed my hands against his chest, his heart thudding beneath my palms.

"Talia," Galen whispered.

I shivered. He had the sexiest voice. I dragged my gaze up and my eyes clashed with his. He wasn't moving, wasn't trying to kiss me, and yet the pull toward him was intense. I was dying to kiss him.

I went up on my toes and closed the distance between our lips, pressing my mouth against his and moaning at the perfection of how it felt when he kissed me back.

Galen's hands slid around my waist, holding me against him.

I parted my lips and welcomed the feel and the taste of his tongue into my mouth.

He kissed me deeply and for so long, I began to get dizzy from a lack of air. But he didn't try and move anything further, and eventually he released my mouth. Both of us panted.

When I finally lifted my head, my eyelids were heavy and I felt partially drugged. "Do we need to leave soon?"

He groaned.

"Unfortunately." He pressed his forehead against mine and sighed. "I'd love to take you upstairs and explore that beautiful body of yours, but we need to get back and warn the pack that nine witches are incoming."

I giggled at the picture he created with his description. "Yeah, I don't think Markus, or Darius, are going to be too pleased to hear that."

Galen chuckled and pulled back from me, as if he didn't want to let go. "You're right. But it's not up to them."

The Alpha was back. I wrapped my arms around my body to stave off the sense of cold left by his withdrawal. I'd been through so much the last few weeks. It had been so nice to be warm and safe and wrapped in Galen's arms. I had forgotten for a few minutes that we had a lot of responsibilities to face. "Anything you need me to get before we go?" I asked him. He shook his head. "Not at all."

He held out his arm and we headed out the door and into the truck. We drove home in relative silence, both of us absorbed in our own thoughts.

When we got back to the pack, I went to help Galen's father at his home while Galen headed off to prepare the rest of the pack for the imminent arrival of the witches.

Eight hours later, they arrived. All nine of them carried several bags each, and were laden with boxes of potions and crystals. They looked like some sort of strange, walking apothecary.

Galen strode up the main road to greet them, but I hung back. I wasn't sure what my role should be, here, and whether I should try to help, or not. This wasn't my pack, after all.

"Talia."

The summons came from above. I turned and craned my neck. The voice had come from the open bedroom window of Galen's father.

"Would you come here, please?"

I ran to the house and entered the Alpha's bedroom.

"Is everything all right, Alpha? What can I get you?"

It turned out he was simply a little hungry, so I made him a light dinner and then, after he'd eaten, I turned on the shower for him. The Alpha hadn't gotten out of bed in a week so, although I was surprised he had the strength to wash, I understood the need.

I put one of the kitchen stools in the shower for him and changed the dirty sheets and bedding while the water ran. Then I rushed back and hung around outside the door in case he needed me. But he managed a rather long shower, dressed himself inside the bathroom, then staggered out again.

I slid under his arm and used my body to help him back to his bed.

He'd even had a shave and looked twenty years younger.

"Oof..." I hefted him onto the bed just as the door opened.

I glanced over my shoulder and couldn't help but giggle at the shocked look on Galen's face. You'd think he'd caught me in bed with his father, naked.

"Everything okay?" I asked him as I pulled back the fresh blankets and lifted his father's legs up and onto the bed.

The Alpha groaned as though in pain, and Galen seemed to snap out of his trance and rush forward. "Do you need help?"

"I think we're okay," I said, then glanced up at the Alpha's pale face. "You pushed yourself a bit much just then."

The Alpha relaxed back against the pillows. "Ah... yeah."

The pain in his expression was intense and I frowned. "Galen, can you stay with your dad? I'm going to get something."

I raced out to the kitchen, and grabbed a glass of milk and some pain killers. I knew he didn't like to take them, but sometimes a reprieve from the body was a good thing.

When I rushed back into the room, I handed him the tablets and the glass of milk, and he swallowed them down without complaint. That alone was testament to the amount of pain he was really in, and a wave of worry washed over me.

"I'll let you sleep," I said, grabbing up the dirty sheets and blankets and balling them in my arms.

I glanced at Galen, silently letting him know his dad really needed rest, then walked out the door.

Galen didn't follow me, and I heard him and his father talking quietly. So, I put on the load of washing, adding extra detergent as the sheets didn't look like they'd been washed in weeks. Longer, even.

By the time I came back to the kitchen, Galen was walking out of his father's room, shutting the door behind him.

"He needs sleep," Galen said, and I nodded. Then he followed me into the kitchen and sat down on the stool.

He blew out a long breath and ran his hand through his hair.

"You okay?" I asked gently.

He met my gaze. "Yeah, I'm okay."

"Then what's troubling you?"

He huffed out a laugh. "The witches. They're already turning things upside down and they've only been here an hour."

"In what way?"

"They don't like the houses we've made available to them. They don't want to share rooms. They wanted dinner, but didn't bring anything with them to cook."

I shook my head. "Sounds like they need a bit of a wake-up call."

They were refugees of a sort. They should be grateful for whatever they were being offered by the pack. I knew I was.

"Maybe some of them could be put in the little cabin where I was, initially?" I suggested. "At least they'd be further away from the main pack."

Galen grinned at me. "I did think of that, and sent four of them out there. There's two bedrooms. They can share."

They certainly could. Or they could magic up some more space.

Come to think of it, they could probably magic up their own dinner if they were that hungry.

"So, what are you going to do?"

Galen got to his feet, pushing up on his arms from the counter. "Tonight? I'm going to bed. It's too late to worry about what I've done now. I've put myself on night shift, so if you hear me sneak out about three a.m., I'm just running with my pack members. Thanks to the witches being here too, I've increased our night-time guard to three men per shift."

I crossed my arms over my chest. "That's gonna stretch you a bit thin. I'd be happy to do some of the running. Are there any other females like me that would help too?"

"Like you?" Galen asked, tilting his head to the side.

"Yeah. Unmated, or at least, no kids. Happy to help."

Galen nodded slowly. "There are, actually. That would help us. Thanks for the advice."

He headed off for a shower and I decided to make a quick batch of raspberry drop cookies, nervous energy still buzzing through my system.

While he was settling into his bed on the couch, I placed a couple of cookies on a plate next to him, with the rest cooling in the kitchen. "See you in the morning."

He stared at me, our gazes locked together. So many unsaid things burned in his eyes and sat heavily between us. Yet, I knew it wasn't the right time to explore any of it. Not yet.

"Good night." I went to my room, showered, and crawled into bed, my body tired but my mind still alive and racing.

Maybe I'd get up with Galen when he left at three a.m. and learn the route they ran around the property. That could be fun.

I closed my eyes and resolved to listen for the moment he left, but the next time I opened my eyes, sunshine streamed in the windows. I'd slept right through to morning.

"Damn. Gonna have to set an alarm for that, in future."

CHAPTER 9
GALEN

"No, Telly, you may not ask a family with three small children to leave the house they built with their own bare hands." I glared down at the redheaded witch who'd had the audacity to ask me to move another family out of their house, because she and her coven sisters 'needed more space'.

Telly glared right back, a strange silver mist floating in her eyes. "Galen, how do you expect us to live like this?"

She gestured around the house to which she'd been assigned. It had been a beautiful home, and yet in the space of a single day, the witches had turned it into what my mother would term, 'a brothel'.

There were clothes and bras and things I couldn't even identify, thrown everywhere. Herbs hung in bunches from the windows, while crystals littered every spare surface.

I crossed my arms over my chest. "I expect you to be grateful for the roof over your head. And if you're not, then I can recommend approaching the Northwood pack next door."

I tilted my head in the direction of Talia's old pack. The witches would be killed on sight if they entered Northwood pack territory, and Telly and I both knew it.

She slammed her lips shut, but there was an angry fire burning in her gaze that made me think this conversation was by no means finished.

Just as I opened my mouth to suggest they clean up the place, the front door to the house swung open and the coven leader, Marguerite, sauntered in.

"Galen, I've set new wards in place for the perimeter of your pack grounds, and had Markus show me where your father's house is."

I turned toward her, my anger at Telly's attitude dissipating at the mention of my dad. "You met the Alpha?"

She shook her head. "Not yet. I simply lay down my strongest ward over and around his house, so that Talia and the Alpha will be the safest if a fight eventuates. Of course, those wards will fall if I'm ever killed, but I believe they will hold firm until that day."

I shivered at her words as a premonition fluttered across my mind. Then it was gone, and I realized it was simply concern for Talia and my father that had sent such an image into my head.

I smiled at the witch. "Thank you for that."

"Your father is sick," Marguerite said, her words not a question. "I sensed it."

I answered her honestly, even though my inclination was to protect my father. "Yes, he is. We haven't been able to identify what's wrong with him."

She nodded, her brow furrowing deeply. "Sarah is the best of us at healing potions. Perhaps I could send her over to see if she can help?"

I inclined my head. "Any help with him would be appreciated."

Marguerite smiled at me and walked me to the door. I ignored Telly, who was still standing across the room, scowling at me.

Once outside, Marguerite took a deep breath and wrapped her shawl tighter around her body. "It's lovely out here, Galen. The ground is sacred, and your people have trust, and love for you. That is a rare thing in this world, but I know with the wolves that love runs deep and true."

Her words bolstered me in a way I couldn't describe, helping to chase away the ghosts of self-doubt that had haunted me through the days since Dad became ill and I'd had to step up.

"My father is a great Alpha."

She nodded and smiled at me. "And you will be, too. You already are."

I snorted. "You're only saying that because I let you into my pack."

The witch's eyes sparkled with a mischievous silver. "That's part of it… definitely. But there's a lot more to this battle that even I know."

I turned to face her properly. "Battle? What do you mean?"

Her smile disappeared. "My instincts are telling me that my witches and I need to put up some better protections on your pack grounds. And on your people. Something's brewing, Galen. Something unsavory, but I can't pinpoint exactly what. You've done a huge favor for us, letting us move in like this, and I feel like we should repay you in some way."

I inclined my head. "Any help you can give us would be appreciated."

This was what I'd hoped for. Support from the witches was one of the main reasons I'd agreed to their request.

I pointed toward the house behind us. "Can you make sure your women stay in line? Harassing my shifter families because your witches want a house to themselves is not... productive. Not for any of us."

It was damn selfish, and ungrateful, but I was trying to be nice so I didn't use those words.

Marguerite inclined her head. "Of course. I will have a word to my sisters."

"Thank you."

A shriek sounded from a house next door to the one we were standing in front of. I shook my head, frustration clawing through me.

Right now, I felt as if this had been a bad idea, but there was no going back now.

And if the witches could help us with strengthening wards, or perhaps even assisting Dad to beat whatever illness ailed him, then a bit of fighting over housing arrangements might be worth the angst.

Another high-pitched shriek sounded, and I rolled my eyes.

Maybe.

Darius was walking down the street toward us, so I lifted my chin and nodded. He didn't respond to my greeting. Instead, the moment he saw I was with Marguerite, he did an abrupt about-face and strode off in the opposite direction. I frowned after him but didn't follow.

Darius didn't like the witches; that had been clear from the moment I'd seen him fighting them in town. His aggression toward them was out of place, and his fear of getting physically close to any one of them was strange.

But the why was unclear. Had he had a run-in with witches in his past that he hadn't told us about? Had he been burned somehow? Or was this hatred of the coven sisters something more?

I took a step in his direction, considering whether to chase him down and ask him directly, but changed my mind as he disappeared around a bend in the road. I wanted to get back to Talia and check on Dad.

I turned away from Marguerite and the various arguments coming from the houses, and headed down the road, back toward my own house. I stopped along the way to talk to a couple of young pack members about some chores I had for them to do later in the week. When I arrived home, the blonde witch Sarah was already standing by the front door.

"Marguerite sent you?" I called out to her as I approached.

Wow. That was quick. We'd only just mentioned it, and here she was, having beaten me back here.

She bobbed her head, seeming shy. "Yes. I was hoping to speak to your father."

I jogged up the steps. "That would be great. Come in."

I opened the door and the witch walked inside my home.

Talia raced out to meet me, as she often did, and stopped abruptly. Her gaze narrowed on the young blonde.

"Talia, this is Sarah. She's good with healing, and she's here to check on Dad and see if there's anything she can suggest."

"Well, he's sleeping," Talia said with a suspicious frown.

"Could I just see him?" Sarah asked, glancing between Talia and myself.

Talia looked up at me, then nodded once when she realized I was okay with it. "I'll show you where he is. Galen, your lunch is on the counter."

The two of them headed upstairs as I sat down and ate. It was strangely comfortable handing over to Talia, and admittedly nice to relax for a few minutes while someone else did my job.

The thought of how much I already trusted Talia shocked me more than I wanted to admit. It was as if she had been in my life—in our pack—for a long time. And it felt good. Right, somehow.

Just as I was finishing up my third turkey roll, Talia and Sarah walked back into the kitchen. They both looked a lot calmer than I expected.

"You two bonded?" I asked with a grin.

Talia rolled her eyes and moved around to the other side of the counter. "Sarah was respectful of the Alpha."

I almost laughed at how protective Talia was over my dad, but then again, she'd just lost her own father and had become my dad's primary carer. It made sense. And I appreciated it, far more than I'd said.

I transferred my attention to the witch. "What can you tell me, Sarah?"

Sarah placed her purple and black tote bag down on the counter and began rummaging through it. "I have some cleansing powder in here. I doubt it will be strong enough to fix whatever's wrong with him, but it might help lessen its hold a little. It will definitely help with some of his pain."

She pulled out a little bottle with a blue liquid in it. "Give him five drops in a jug of water every day, until I can find a way to diagnose him properly. I'll come back tomorrow with more equipment, if that's all right with you?"

I nodded slowly. A correct diagnosis was vital in figuring out how to heal my dad.

"I'll take that," Talia said, holding out her hand for the bottle.

Without question, Sarah handed over the medicine. "It might taste a little tart to him, and that's okay. It's very mild, so won't do him any harm."

Talia wrapped her fingers around the bottle and held it tightly.

"Thank you," I said. "You are welcome to come back tomorrow."

Sarah smiled. "Yeah, I'd like that. Thank you."

She bobbed her head and left, leaving Talia and I alone in the room.

Talia exhaled loudly, like she was exhausted.

"You okay?" I asked her.

"Yeah. I'm just worried about everything and everyone. The pack, the witches, your dad, you. It's all just a mess at the moment, isn't it?"

I pressed my hands into the cool countertop. "Yeah, it is."

Sure felt like a mess to me.

"Tell me more about the witches," Talia said. "Are they being really painful?"

I couldn't stop the sudden laugh that bubbled up. "Oh, yeah. A right pain in the ass."

I spend the next hour telling Talia little stories about what had happened when the witches arrived last night, and what they'd gotten up to already this morning. Almost everyone the witches had come into contact with so far had had their noses put out of joint, it seemed.

By the end of the debrief, I felt the heavy weight of the world lifting off my shoulders. "Thanks for the chat," I said as I stood up, "but I need to get back to it."

Talia smiled at me and picked up the plate I'd left in front of me. "I'll be here. You can vent to me anytime. See you at dinner."

I thanked her again and left, feeling unusually happy. Despite the situation we were in, Talia made me feel content on a bone-deep level.

Markus came running up to me as soon as I exited my front door. I sighed, expecting another petty witch complaint.

"More demon attacks in town."

The shock hit me like a punch to my guts. "What the hell?" I pulled my truck keys out of my pocket. "Who did they attack?"

"I heard it was some of the humans this time. Scaring them, setting houses on fire."

"Oh, for fuck's sake." I stalked over to my truck.

Markus ran up to me and grabbed me by the arm. "They're gone now, by all accounts. There's no reason to go in."

I slid my keys back into my jean pocket. "That's good, I suppose. But what does this even mean? I don't understand what they want. Other than causing chaos and mayhem. There doesn't seem any rhyme or reason to it."

At least none of the guys could say it had anything to do with Talia. She was safely inside my father's house, and the demons had come nowhere near us.

"I don't either, Galen. But I think you should close the bar for a couple of weeks. The guys are getting tired. Between shifts at the bar, running extra security around here at night..."

He trailed off, and I groaned.

"You're right. I'll drive in tonight and put up the signs myself."

"Thanks." Markus clapped me on the shoulder and walked away.

I hadn't closed my bar for more than a long weekend, for... well, ever. I didn't take holidays and I had a loyal team on board. This was totally unforeseen. But Markus was correct. I didn't need to be at my apartment at the moment, nor did I need the stress of work. Right now, I needed to focus on my pack, my people, the witches, my dad, and Talia, and ensure everyone under my protection remained safe.

Because only God knew what was coming for us next.

CHAPTER 10
TALIA

Sarah returned as promised the next day and performed some spells on the Alpha. She placed pink crystals in his room and invoked an incantation, while I watched carefully to ensure he remained safe. I had made sure he drank all his detox water the night before, and readied another jug for today.

By the time Sarah finished her spellcasting, the crystals had turned from pink to a smoky black color. She studied them closely, a worried look bringing her brows together.

"What's wrong?" I asked, the moment we stepped out of the Alpha's bedroom.

"He's sick," she said.

I stared at her. Was she crazy? "Ah, yeah. Stating the obvious, much?"

She shook her head, seeming distracted, so I directed her into the kitchen and pulled out the leftover roast chicken I'd made for dinner last night. "Are you hungry?"

"Yes, that would be great, thanks." Sarah slid onto a stool and picked up another pink crystal from her bag. "These are healing crystals. They aren't very strong, but you saw what happened to them after only an hour in the Alpha's room."

"He did that to them?" I asked, pulling out plates and grabbing some tomatoes and spinach from the fridge.

"If you mean turning the crystals black, then yeah. He's... sick," she repeated, and this time I noted her extreme concern.

I pushed a plate of chicken salad at her and picked up my fork. "You keep saying that. We know he's sick. What aren't you saying?"

Sarah bit her lip. She looked about twenty years old, which made me think it would be nice to have someone around who was my age and wasn't terrified of me.

"Come on, Sarah. Just say it."

"He's dying." She burst out with the revelation and my heart skipped a beat. "He's not just sick, he's dying, and I'm not sure why. None of the spells I cast told me anything, other than the fact that he doesn't have a lot of time left."

I sucked in a deep breath and let it out slowly. "I know. I've been feeling it, too. But I don't know what to do for him, other than try to keep his pain under control and give him as much support and care as he wants."

"I can give him more potions, pain killers, and detoxes. It might help to slow the process. But until we know what's causing him to spiral downwards, I can't do anything else."

I sighed. "Thank you for everything you've tried so far, Sarah. It is much appreciated."

We ate our chicken in silence after that, and once we were done, I quickly washed up and then went to check on the Alpha. He was fast asleep and seemed to be breathing easier than he had been earlier. Maybe the detox was helping. At least a little.

"I've gotta run a few errands," I said to Sarah. "Pick up

some food for the Alpha. That kind of thing. Wanna come along for the walk?"

Her face lit up. "Sure! I'd love to get out and explore a bit more of the town."

I liked Sarah. She was good company, and as we walked around town, collecting fresh eggs, bread, and muffins, we chatted about life, and magic, and working at the restaurant in town.

I missed Kylie and the others who worked there, but it was just too dangerous to go in and see them now. I hoped they were all still okay.

"I better head back, but thanks for the chat." I clung tight to my basket of goodies with one hand, and waved goodbye to Sarah with the other. "I enjoyed your company."

She smiled shyly. "Me too." She turned away, then back again. "Would you mind if I came back tomorrow? I've had an idea and I want to try something else."

"Sure." I watched her leave, and then returned to the Alpha's house.

The Alpha called out for me the moment I stepped inside.

"Hey Talia! Could I get something to eat?"

I glanced at the clock. It was too late for lunch but too early for dinner. His sleep had thrown things out a little, but I was glad he'd felt able to rest for so long. That was surely a good sign. I hoped.

"Of course, Alpha! I'll be right in."

He rarely asked for food. I was usually the one forcing him to eat. I put together a plate of cheese, ham, tomatoes, and fresh slices of bread slathered with butter.

When I took it in to him and placed it on his lap, he was looking brighter than he ever had, to my eyes.

"You're looking well." I stared at his warmer-than-usual complexion in surprise.

"I feel well," he said, picking up a piece of ham and eating it with gusto. "Not sure what that blonde witch did, but it definitely helped."

Shock held me rigid, but I forced a smile to my face. The spells and crystals—or maybe it was the detox drops—were really working!

"Sarah wasn't sure she did anything right, but obviously she did. Alpha, I'm..." I swallowed hard. "I'm really glad to see you looking like this."

He grinned at me and proceeded to eat everything on his plate with an appetite I'd never seen on him.

I turned away to get him another glass of detox water and tried hard not to cry. I would have loved to meet Galen's father a few years ago, when he was a normal Alpha: strong and fit, running about town. For the first time, I could see traces of that man, and it brought home to me how unwell he had been, up to now.

The man I had known so far was frail and bedbound. It wasn't right.

When Galen arrived home that night, he seemed more stressed than normal.

"Hey, are you okay?" I asked, once he'd finished the pie one of the neighbors had brought by for him.

He shrugged. "Yeah. Closed down the bar indefinitely, today. First time ever. It was a bit... strange."

I felt his sadness so strongly, it was as though the emotions coursed over me in waves. "I'm so sorry. I hope it won't be for long."

He sighed and took the plate around to the sink to wash up. "Yeah, hopefully not."

"Your dad ate a large meal this afternoon. He looked much better after Sarah's visit and a long nap," I said, hoping to cheer him up.

He shot me a quick, surprised grin, and then hurried upstairs.

He returned a few minutes later. "I looked in on him, but he was sleeping. He did seem to have a bit of color in his cheeks, though, which is good."

Galen sat on the couch, seeming less stressed than when he'd first arrived home. I busied myself finishing the clearing up, and once everything was done, I sat at the opposite end of the couch to him, with the TV playing some drama. I wasn't giving any attention to it. I was too aware of Galen. Where he was, how he moved, even how he smelt. Everything about him both excited me and made me a little afraid. Of myself more than anything else. He was too much of everything. Too brave, too courageous, too hot, too sweet.

Far too Alpha for the likes of me.

I wanted to reach across the expanse of space that separated us and touch him, to feel the warmth of him against me once again. But I didn't know if I had earned that right. In the end, I kept my hands to myself.

"How was your day?" He turned toward me.

"Good. Actually, as I mentioned, Sarah was here for a while, and then she walked with me while I picked up the food orders for your dad. I like her, Galen." It was surprisingly nice to have made a new friend in this strange world in which I'd found myself.

Galen smiled at me. "That's great. I'm glad you've made friends with one of the witches. Having powerful allies is always a good idea."

I hadn't really thought about it like that. "Yeah, I guess. For me, it's just nice having someone my own age to talk to."

During the day, I rarely saw anyone but the Alpha, and he slept a lot.

"Do you wanna come closer?" Galen asked, lifting his arm and indicating I could cuddle into him, if I wanted.

Did I want? Of course, I did! I pressed my lips tight so that I didn't give myself away by squealing with excitement and scooted across the couch cushions so that I was sitting next to him.

He placed his arm around me and tucked me into his side.

I put my head down onto his shoulder and sighed as his body heat and a sense of protection enfolded me.

"You know..." he began, and I closed my eyes against the wave of pleasure that passed over me when he spoke. His voice had such a melodic effect on me.

"Yeah?" I prompted when he stopped.

"I know everything that's happened to you recently has been horrible, so I don't want this to come out the wrong way."

I tried not to laugh at the awkwardness in his tone. He was clearly trying to tell me something positive, but possibly going about it in a backwards way. Galen was thirty-ish and an Alpha wolf, yet he could be so bashful sometimes. I loved it.

"Okay. I'll try not to take it that way," I said with a grin.

"I'm glad you're here," he said in a low growl. "With me."

I sat up so I could look straight at him. I wanted him to see my sincerity. "Me too."

He cupped my face and kissed me. Softly at first, then harder, deeper, until I was pressed into his chest and gasping, needing to get closer. Desperate for more.

He pulled back and tugged on my waist. "Jump up. Straddle me."

I didn't wait to allow any embarrassment to rise. I just jumped up onto my knees and swung a leg over his hips, wanting to kiss him for as long as he'd let me.

I slid my arms around his neck and met his lips with mine, moaning at the pleasure, the rightness of this connection.

He slipped one hand beneath my t-shirt, sliding around my waist and up my back.

When he flicked open my bra, I gasped against his mouth, then pressed in deeper as his fingers fluttered across my skin. My eyes closed again as I sunk into the pleasure his touch evoked.

His hands came around the front of me, cupping my freed breasts almost reverently, softly, his thumbs flicking over my taut nipples until heat poured through me.

I grabbed tight to his hair, wanting more.

"Galen!" the Alpha called out, and I jumped.

Galen's hands stilled, and I slid off his lap and stood in one fast move.

Galen stayed seated, his eyes smoldering with the heat of unmistakable passion. His lips were still parted and red from my kisses.

I giggled at the sight of him so obviously aroused, then covered my mouth with my hand. I probably looked exactly the same.

But at least the Alpha hadn't called for me.

Galen's lips tweaked up into a rueful grin. "Yeah, Dad. Coming!"

He got to his feet and adjusted his jeans, the bulge beneath the zipper more obvious than either of us would like his father to be aware of.

"Great timing, huh?"

I smiled softly. I was kind of enjoying all these great kissing sessions we were having. Made me want him even more.

"Should I wait up for you, or...?"

Galen glanced in the direction of his dad's room, then back at me. "I've actually got a few pack business things to discuss with him, so maybe you should head to bed."

Then his eyes lit up with a teasing light I knew well. "Do you want me to join you in there?"

I reached out and grabbed for his hand. "Think you can keep your hands to yourself?"

He chuckled. "Nope."

I didn't want to reject him, but with the advantage of a few minutes off his lap, my brain had switched back on again and I realized I wasn't ready for more yet. So I lifted his hand and kissed his fingers. "Maybe another night?"

His eyes sobered, but I could tell he understood. There was no malice or anger in his gaze.

"Definitely," he said, and I shivered at the promise in the word.

I pressed a chaste kiss to his lips, then stepped back, parts of me aching that had never ached so badly before. "Goodnight, Galen."

He growled a little, shook his head, then walked off.

I ran to my room, a hysterical laugh hovering on my lips. At least I knew for sure he wanted me, and that was an amazing thing in this new, unknown world.

Everything else was as solid as water, impossible to hold, and just as easy to slip through my fingers.

CHAPTER 11
GALEN

I tossed and turned through the night, dozing in between fits of being wide awake. God, I wanted Talia. But the ramifications of what that would mean, for her and for me, were too much to comprehend at this moment.

It was both a help and a hindrance that my dad liked and trusted her so much. It softened me too much knowing he thoroughly approved of the woman who'd once been destined to be a rival Alpha's mate.

I rolled over yet again, trying to resist the urge to punch my pillow in frustration. A warning howl came through my window. The sound hit me like a shot. I jumped up off the couch and ran for the front door, yanking it open. The protection wards rippled around me.

Someone gasped behind me. Talia had woken up, alerted, as my whole pack would be, to whatever danger was coming for us.

The wards rippled again. It felt like they'd been punched.

Whatever was coming was big and no doubt deadly.

"Talia! Stay here with Dad!" I yelled over my shoulder, praying she'd do as she was told, then jumped off the porch, shifting mid-air and landing with my paws on the grass.

Down the street, men ran out of their homes, and even the women were shifting too, ready to protect their children if it came to it.

Black and gray wolves fell in behind me as I raced the length of our main street. I met up with Markus, who was bleeding, his right eye damaged and his ear ripped off.

I didn't bother shifting back so we could speak properly. I had a small amount of telepathy with my wolves, especially my Betas.

More feelings than true words.

But Markus was communicating, and I tuned in hard to listen.

Talia's old pack. We're under attack.

I stared hard at Markus. That sounded bad, but why was there a note of fear in the air around his non-verbal communication? We had taken on the Northwood pack before and won.

I cocked my head, asking the silent question of Markus.

It's not just them. They have vampires with them.

Vampires? It was rare for vamps and wolves to fight together. Someone must have worked a deal, or perhaps even magic of some kind, to get the vampires on their side.

Fuck.

I growled low, then turned and vocalized my orders to my men via barking, growling, and projecting instructions into their minds. Thank God for telepathy.

Be careful. Surround and protect the town. And know this is possibly a fight to the death. Chase off anyone who doesn't belong. Watch out for the vampires. Rip off their heads if you want them to stay down.

We took off, circling the town and putting ourselves between the coming enemy and our home.

Maddox's pack had breached our perimeter and were already in our forest, rows of beady yellow eyes glaring at us as they stalked forward through the brush.

I halted, waiting for them to emerge into the open space between our town and the forest edge. This was our home turf, and we had the advantage. Let them come to us.

My pack stopped too, taking the lead from me.

The enemy wolves emerged, spread out and snarling. Behind them stood several vampires—master level by the look of at least one of them. My hackles rose. I lowered my head, readying, and watched as a red haze misted over the lead vampire's eyes.

So much for the peace treaty I'd made with the Northwood pack.

There was a moment of hesitation, of each side weighing up the other, and then the wolves charged. I launched myself at the nearest black wolf and landed on top of his back. I tore at his fur and flesh, ripping a hole in his shoulder, before he managed to shake me off.

Howls and grunts rose as the sounds of battle intensified around me. I had no time to consider anything, except launch, attack, evade.

My mouth filled with hot wolf blood as I bit and ripped into them. I came face to face with a huge wolf—it wasn't Maddox but it must have been one of his Betas—and our lips lifted in a snarl before we were on each other.

He managed to claw at my hind leg before I got him by the throat. I sank my teeth deep, holding on and shaking him, until the growling snarls turned to a whimper. I dropped him to the ground, hardly even noticing when he slunk away almost on his stomach.

Another one down. How many to go?

I risked a glance around. In every direction, wolves engaged in deadly combat.

Some of the younger women in my pack had shifted and were rushing in to help. Equal parts pride and worry filled my chest. I scanned their ranks, praying Talia had obeyed my demand to stay with my dad and that she hadn't shifted and decided to join the fight.

I couldn't see her among the smaller female wolves, thank God, and my heart thudded in relief. At least I knew she was still likely behind the protective wards in my dad's house. One less person to worry about.

My Betas, meanwhile, were right in the thick of it.

On my right, Tommy was engaged with one of the vampires. His lip was raised, and his vicious snarls rose above the sounds of battle as he stared down the vampire with the red gaze. I trusted Tommy in that match-up. If anyone could take out a vamp and survive, it was Tommy.

Beyond him, David was facing off with a Northwood shifter. They were evenly matched in size and weight, but David was a master at fighting and I sensed he would be okay.

On my left, several feet away, Markus fought two shifters at once. I started over to help him but an attack on my flank diverted my attention. I was pulled back into my own skirmish until I managed to fight yet another shifter off.

There seemed to be too many of them. Where had they all come from?

My men—and my women—were strong, but we were outnumbered in this, and many of the vampires still stood waiting, as if they intended to swoop in at the end.

My gaze clashed with the master vampire, and a haze of red filled his vision.

He wanted to kill me, badly. And with the adrenaline of battle rushing through my veins, who was I to deny him?

I leaped over the head of a snapping wolf and landed directly in front of the lead vamp. He took a tiny step back, as if he hadn't expected that from me, and then grinned.

"Ready to die, wolf?"

I didn't bother with an answer, but simply lifted my lip and showed him my teeth, before launching straight up at his scrawny pale neck.

He was lightning fast, though, dodging away from my snapping jaw, before jumping onto my back. I twirled and shook, trying to dislodge him, but he had engaged his taloned nails and hung on for grim death, no matter how hard I tried.

I dropped to the ground and rolled. That got him off me, but then he was back in my face, hissing, his fangs fully extended and red blood lust in his eyes.

"You need to die, but not before I suck you dry, wolf."

He sprang at me again, so fast he was a blur even with my shifter vision. I felt the pain of a bite on my neck. I tipped back my head and howled.

It was a howl of rage more than anything else, but not one I expected to be answered.

A blast of silver light almost blinded me, and the pain in my neck disappeared.

I turned my head to see Marguerite and Telly, with several other witches, running toward the battle ground.

Marguerite shot me a glance and nodded. It had been her stream of blast magic that had dislodged the vamp off my back.

She and Telly turned and stood, back-to-back, and began

blasting streams of silver out into the battle. Other witch pairs did the same.

I had to trust that they knew what they were doing and would only harm the Northwood invaders or the vamps, and not members of my own pack.

I would thank the witches later, if we all survived. For now, the battle was still raging.

There were rogue vamps, and enemy wolves, to destroy.

CHAPTER 12
TALIA

The sounds of a huge battle raged outside, and my wolf clamored inside my chest to burst free. But I'd promised Galen I would stay with the Alpha.

"Talia! What's happening?" the Alpha's voice rang out.

I ran to his bedroom and sat down on the chair next to him, even though I could barely stay still. I was jumping out of my skin, but he needed me.

"We're being attacked. Galen and his Betas have gone to defend the town." I shivered as I spoke.

"Who is it?" the Alpha asked, narrowing his eyes at me.

"I don't know." I said, shaking my head. "It could be my old pack, but... I honestly don't know."

It was the truth. Strange sensations rippled over my skin, as if there was some kind of magic in the air. It may have been my old pack, but if so, they had brought more than their wolf shifters to this fight.

The Alpha threw back the covers. "I need to get out there."

"No way!" I pushed on his chest, pressing him back into

bed. He was weak enough that it was easy for me to hold him in place. "You can't do that. If something happened to you, Galen would kill me."

The Alpha glared at me. "Well, I can't just sit here and do nothing."

I pressed a hand into my temple. Think. Think. How could I stay here and protect the Alpha, but help at the same time?

Then I had it. "Your house has the best wards in the whole town. We should get as many people in here as we can. The older women. The children. The vulnerable ones who can't fight. You and your house can protect them, Alpha, if Galen and his men fail."

As long as the witches weren't killed, they would be safe in this house, too.

The Alpha's eyes lit up. "Go. Get them. Now."

I rushed out of his room and into the street. I looked left and right, but where did I even start? Next door!

I ran to their front door. "Norah! It's Talia. Come out. Quick."

The Alpha's neighbor opened the door, her eyes wide with fear. I could tell she already knew we were under attack. "What is it, Talia?"

"The Alpha's home has the best warded protection. The witches have surrounded his house with shields. Come. He wants everyone inside his house, now."

Norah nodded, grim determination taking over her expression. "I'll take this side of the town, you go down that way, toward the south. Knock on every door."

I nodded, and then bolted to the next house, glad to have someone else to help with the task.

Between us, Norah and I called every woman, child, and elderly or frail pack member, and soon there was a stream of people rushing toward the Alpha's house. It wasn't a huge space, but they'd fit.

When I reached the final house, where a woman named Abigail lived with her four children, I gathered up her baby in my arms. "Go, Abigail! Go! I'm following you!"

The snarls and howls rising everywhere around us were terrifying. Some of the women had shifted into protector mode as I knocked at their doors, but had shifted back when I told them the plan.

I ran for the Alpha's house with Abigail's baby in my arms. The heat of danger prickled along my spine. The tingle of menace erupted in my brain.

This wasn't just an attack by wolf shifters.

There were demons around. I could sense them.

This was very bad.

The front door was open and I hurried up the porch, yelling to everyone gathering inside. "There's the back bedroom, too. Spread out. Get comfortable."

"You can come up here too, children." the Alpha called out down the stairs, and I exchanged a smile with a nearby woman I hadn't met. Relief filled her gaze.

"Yes," I told the little ones, all clinging to their mother's legs. "Go up and see your Alpha. He'll tell you a story. I'm going to go check on your dads."

Norah grabbed my arm. "No, Talia. Stay."

I shook my head. "I need to check on the witches, and get them here too, if I can. You all stay here. The wards are strong. Be safe. I won't be long."

I took off down the street in the direction of the witches' houses.

Someone behind me called out my name, loud and long, in a sing-song voice.

My heart sank.

I swiveled around and saw him. Maddox. He was naked, obviously having shifted back from being in his wolf form. Blood ran down his neck from some kind of small wound, but otherwise, he looked healthy and strong.

Surprisingly so. Had he not participated in the battle?

Then I did a double-take. The red glimmer of a demon's influence shimmered in Maddox's eyes.

Oh, God. Maddox was mean enough, but with a demon riding him as well?

He rushed closer and I held my breath, trying to control the fear.

"You disloyal little slut." He spat at me.

My mouth dropped open. A slut? Seriously? I'd been kissed three times by Galen, after Maddox had rejected me and thrown me out of my own home.

Who was the disloyal one in that scenario?

"Have you opened your legs for that feral new Alpha?" He sneered. "I bet you have. Has he got between those thighs that refused to open for me?"

"Refused… You're insane." And he was. Delusional at best. He'd twisted everything good and made it something crazy. "You're the one who wanted to wait!"

I couldn't believe I was trying to reason with him in this moment. I mentally shook my head at my own actions. Leave him, and run, I told myself. But something stayed my legs.

I'd been desperate to know what physical love felt like, with Maddox. He was the one who'd never wanted to enjoy me in that way.

"Bitch." He began to growl. I could feel the ripple in the air that meant he was about to shift. He would attack me, then, for sure. Which meant I only had one option.

Despite my promise to Galen, I had to shift myself.

"You're going to die." He spoke through sharpened teeth that had already begun the shift. The red of his eyes intensified. "There's no-one around to save you now."

I pulled forth my own shifter as fast I could, my clothes tearing into shreds as my wolf leapt forward into freedom.

He leapt for me, his huge jaw crashing together in a bite that just missed my head.

He was so much bigger than me, and stronger, but I was faster. Thank God.

I weaved and ducked around him as he launched and bit and swiped at me with his clawed paws.

I couldn't keep this up forever, but I had no choice. It was fight or die.

I darted in, scoring a quick bite on his right hind leg. He swirled and landed a bite of his own on my front leg before I managed to dance out of reach. The snarling that erupted from his throat had an added sinister quality that I suspected came from whatever demon was influencing him.

It was terrifying, knowing I was facing down not only a crazed ex, but one who was most likely being controlled by a demon.

He lunged at me again, and I darted back. I slipped on the gravel in the road, and he was on me before I could recover.

The weight of him crushed me down onto the ground and I couldn't breathe, couldn't think, beyond the terror of knowing this might be the moment I die.

I heard a crack and pain flared through me. He'd just damaged a couple of my ribs.

Then he raised his head, staring into my eyes, and the swirling red shifted, as if he wasn't quite sure what to do next. It was only for a second or two. But the pause was long enough for me to snatch at hope. I craned my neck, reaching up and ignoring the pain of my broken ribs, and snapped my jaws shut on his throat.

He yelped and jumped off me. I hung on tight, coming with him and hanging off his neck as he stood and tried to shake me off.

His hot blood filled my mouth, trickling down my throat and threatening to choke me, but still I refused to let go.

Hold on, or he'll kill me.

An almighty shake from his broad frame dislodged me, and I flew through the air to land on a patch of grass.

The breath was completely knocked out of me, and so much pain rushed in that I thought I might lose consciousness.

His throat was ripped badly, and he gave me a shocked look, before turning and loping away into the shadows, leaving a trail of blood in his wake.

I lay on my side and struggled to draw in shallow breaths, unable to believe that I somehow had just bested my ex, the Alpha's son of the Northwood pack.

And with a demon host on board him, as well.

The urge to find Galen and make sure he was safe almost overwhelmed me.

I let the shift fade, rippling away until I lay in my human form, shivering on the ground and trying not to pass out.

Somehow, I struggled to my feet, my arms wrapped around my aching middle, and began to stagger back toward the Alpha's house.

I needed clothes, and then I needed to go find Galen.

Abigail, the shifter whose baby I'd carried earlier, rushed out into the street to meet me. She was carrying a set of clothes, which she helped me into because I was beyond trying to dress myself.

"Oh my God, Talia," she said. "I thought you were going to die. Come back to the house and let us help you."

"Thank you," I whispered. "But I have to find Galen, wherever he is."

Was he even still alive?

What the heck was going on lately?

Had everyone and everything in this world been driven mad by an influx of demons?

CHAPTER 13
TALIA

I staggered around a bend in the road and found Sarah tending to one of Galen's Betas, Tommy. He was sitting on the street, and by the look of the blood pooled around him, had been injured quite badly.

"What can I do to help?" I asked Sarah as I wobbled up to them.

My legs felt like Jell-O, but at least they still worked. Sort of.

"You can help me lift... oh my God, Talia!" Sarah stared at me. "What happened to you?"

I shrugged off her concern. "I'm okay. Just got into a fight with an ex."

"Maddox?" Tommy's voice was a croak as he piped up from his position on the ground. "I hope you killed the bastard."

Worry coursed through me as I saw how much blood soaked Tommy's chest and abdomen. I met Sarah's gaze, and wordlessly she nodded. Tommy's injury was bad.

I looked back down at him. "The gutless wonder ran off when I started kicking his ass," I joked.

Tommy chuckled, then groaned.

I stood straighter, my ribs still painful, but they would heal in time. Tommy needed help now.

"What can I do, Sarah?"

She looked me up and down. "Internal injuries for you, too?"

I nodded. "A couple of broken ribs, I think. Nothing punctured. I'm good."

Sarah pulled a vial out of her purse. "Drink this. It tastes disgusting but will help."

I didn't even question her. I just unstoppered the vial and tossed it back.

She was right about the taste—like dirt and bile and all gross things. But within seconds of the liquid going down my throat, the intense pain in my side began to subside.

"Wow. Thank you. Now. How can I help?"

"I need to move him inside. Can we get him to the nearest house?" She pointed to Tommy, who tried to get up and then sank back, half-laying on the ground.

I nodded and looked around. Abigail's place was just across the street. "We can go there," I said. "Can you give him something for the pain? Or do I need to sew something together before we move him?"

Sarah assessed him. "No sewing here, but you're right. He's gonna need pain killers." She searched in her bag, then pulled out a red vial. "This might help."

She handed the little bottle to Tommy, who followed my lead and swallowed it down without question. He groaned and sagged. The small amount of color that had remained in his face drained out, and fast.

"He looks worse!"

"We need to move him quickly," Sarah said.

"Come on, Tommy."

I bent down and put my arms around his body. He was big, but I was a shifter, and Sarah did some kind of incantation that seemed to give both of us a surge of energy. She stepped in to his other side.

"Can you get your legs under you?" I asked him.

He nodded, and then groaned as we hauled him to his feet.

Blood gushed down his thigh from a laceration in his groin. "We've gotta move quick."

We staggered across into Abigail's house and managed to get him on the kitchen table. There, the two of us worked on him with haste. I stitched and held flesh together while Sarah cast spells and poured stinky solutions over his body.

"What the hell happened here?" I asked Tommy, as I moved up to his shoulder where there was a huge chunk of flesh missing out of his deltoid.

"Vampire," Tommy whispered, turning paper-white.

"I think we're losing him," I said in a panicked voice.

Sarah studied his face.

"No. It's just the pain. You can pass out, Tommy. We've got you," she said, before continuing to work on him.

I glanced down his body. Sarah was right. His wounds were beginning to heal already, the stitches I'd just given him holding. His bleeding was slowing down.

"You're going to be okay," I told him. "Pass out if you can. Let your body rest. You'll heal faster."

He nodded, then touched my hand.

"Yes, Tommy?"

He was moving his lips as though whispering, but I couldn't hear him. I moved closer and put my ear next to his lips.

"I was wrong about you," he said. "This isn't your fault."

I stood up straighter and smiled down at him. "Thanks."

His eyes closed and his head fell to the side.

I put my fingers to the pulse in his neck, finding it weak, but still beating.

"What did he say?" Sarah asked, as she waved her hands one more time over his chest.

"That this wasn't my fault," I said, staring down at the vampire bite. I had no idea how to heal it. "But part of me thinks it is."

Sarah gaped at me. "Seriously?"

"Well, the pack that attacked us were my old pack," I admitted, not looking at her.

There was silence, then she said, "Yeah, but did you see the demon influence? Red eyes all over the place. And those vampires that fought with them? That's not a natural pairing, Talia. Shifters and vamps don't play nice together, usually."

She frowned. "None of this was your fault, and it's not like they came for you."

"It's definitely not your fault." Galen's voice came from behind us.

I swiveled around to find him standing in the doorway.

Tears pricked at my eyes. He was alive. I fought the urge to run at him and jump into his arms.

"If I hadn't..."

"No, Talia," he said, stepping into the house just as the sun rose and light filtered in around him. "Your old pack attacked us first, days before I found you, and that event started all of this."

I nodded, tears gathering momentum and threatening to fall.

I sniffed loudly, calling them back in. "Why do I always end up crying around you? It's not fair. I'm pretty tough until I see you walk in the door."

He smiled.

"I'll take it as a compliment." He stepped up and pressed a kiss to my hair. "I'm so glad you're okay. I've heard from several people already how brave you were in fighting off that asshole, Maddox. I'm proud of you, Talia."

He was proud of me? My heart swelled in my chest and a silly grin creased my face. "I'm glad you're okay, too, Galen, and we're all proud of you."

Sarah's gaze slid between us, but she didn't say anything.

"How's the pack?" I asked him.

Galen sighed and his brows came together. "We've lost quite a few people. And there's a lot who need healing." He nodded at Tommy. "How's my Beta doing?"

Sarah wiped her hands clean on a towel nearby and handed it to me to do the same.

I didn't know what to tell him about Tommy. "Well..."

"He'll be okay," Sarah said. "Thanks to some luck, a bit of magic, his own healing ability, and Talia's sewing skills, he'll be fine."

Galen's lips kicked up a little at the sides when he looked at me. "Yeah, I know, she's good at sewing flesh together. There are a lot of people who could use your help. Are either of you up to more healing?"

"Yes! Of course," I said, the pain in my ribs only slightly twitching inside my chest. "I want to help."

My run-in with Maddox had solidified how separate I was to my old pack now. It was almost a waste to even call them my old pack.

The Northwood pack were nothing to me. Not anymore.

Galen's pack was my pack now, and standing with them today, fighting against Maddox, had really reminded me how loyal I now was to Galen and his people.

Sarah followed us, and together we went out into the street, daylight upon us. We traveled from house to house, helping the injured how and where we could. The other witches helped with the healing, too, and went in and out of various houses along the streets. When we reached the end of the stretch of houses on the main street, Galen put out his hand to stop me.

"I think it's time you went back to Dad's."

I rubbed my hands together, feeling itchy, sweaty, and in need of a shower after having so much blood on me today. "All right. What are you going to do?"

"I'm going to help with the burials." His tone was grave, and my heart went out to him.

What a horrible thing to have to do for members of his pack. His people.

"I'm so sorry."

He nodded. "It's the last thing I can do for them."

I had to touch him, to reassure myself that he truly was okay. I stepped closer and went up on my toes so that I could press my lips to his.

I stood there, feeling his heat against mine as we kissed, then I stepped back. "I'll go and check on your dad. We hid all the women and children in his house, to give them the best chance with the protective wards in place."

Galen's face lit up. "That was really smart."

I reached for his hand and squeezed his fingers. "I'll see you later. Okay?"

He nodded. "See you then."

I turned and walked home, my heart going out to him, for what he now had to do. Bury some of his family.

When I got back, Norah was the only one still sitting in the living room. All the others had gone.

"Talia! Are you okay?"

"Yeah, I'm fine, why... oh." I glanced down at the clothes Abigail had given me after my fight with Maddox. The long yellow summer dress was now covered in blood. "It's not my blood. I've been helping to heal some of the other pack members."

Norah nodded, looking wan and exhausted. "Since you're back, I might leave. The Alpha has been quiet."

"How did it go here?"

She walked to the door. "We watched your fight with that large male wolf. You've got some go in you."

"Thanks, Norah. And thanks for staying with the Alpha."

She nodded and left.

I shut the door and exhaled slowly. Fuck. What a night!

"Talia. Is that you?" the Alpha called from upstairs.

"Yes, Alpha!" I headed into his bedroom, where he was sitting up in his bed. "Can I get you something to eat? Or drink?"

He shook his head. "No. Not at all. I've had a dozen women here for five hours. I'm full."

I chuckled. "I imagine you would be. Do you mind if I go have a quick shower? I definitely need it."

I indicated the mess I wore and backed toward the door.

"Talia."

"Yes, Alpha?"

"You should call me Max."

I blinked at him. "Alpha Max?"

He chuckled. "No. You can call me just Max, if you want. Or Dad, if that suits you better."

My nose tingled with impending tears. "But... I..."

"I'm not pushing, at all, but I know you and Galen are... close. It doesn't seem right that you wait on me day and night, and still call me Alpha."

I put my hand to my chest, over my heart which was fluttering fast. I'd never had such acceptance before. "Oh, Alpha, I...."

"Max," he corrected. "Or Dad."

I swallowed hard. I didn't want to insult him, but Galen and I weren't mated, and I'd only lost my father a few weeks ago. "Could we start with Max? And depending on what happens in the future..."

He inclined his head. "That sounds like a good compromise."

I laughed, feeling slightly hysterical, probably due to exhaustion. "Thank you, Max. Well, I'm going to have a shower and rest a little, maybe. But if you need me, call out, okay?"

My body was truly aching now that I'd slowed down. The ribs were making themselves felt once again.

"Go shower and rest. I'll still be here."

I smiled, as I ducked out and headed toward my bedroom.

The shower was pure bliss, hot water to wash away the stench of battle and the blood of my injured pack.

Once I was clean, my body ached so much I ended up crawling into bed and sleeping for a few hours. When I woke, a lot of my surface injuries were healed and my ribs were barely an ache around my middle. I wanted to see what had happened to the rest of the pack, so I jumped out of bed and dressed.

But, by the time I'd made Max some lunch, Galen staggered back home.

"Come in, come in." I opened the front door and encouraged him inside. "Food or shower first?"

"Definitely a shower." He stumbled inside and hit the wall.

"Galen! That you, son?" Max called out.

"Yeah, Dad. Give me a minute. I've really gotta shower." Galen pushed himself forward, and into the main bathroom off the end of the hall. He could barely stand up and I couldn't bring myself to just watch him.

I raced down the hall and stepped into the bathroom with him. "Let me help you."

I twisted the taps, the shower head blasting out cold water, then warming up while I adjusted the temperature.

He wasn't wearing a shirt, but he pushed his jeans down his thighs and stepped out of them before moving into the cubicle. He was bruised and battered, dirty and bloody.

"Can I..." I didn't finish my sentence, because I shouldn't be asking.

Galen could barely move, and I needed to confirm that he was not about to keel over.

I tugged off the tank and denim shorts I'd only put on an hour ago, and got rid of my underwear.

Then I stepped into the shower behind Galen's massive body and picked up the soap. "Do you mind if I help you?"

I set the soap in the center of Galen's back and began to run it in massive circles, helping the dirt and grime to dislodge.

"You know this isn't fair." He groaned, reaching out and pushing his palm into the tile and hanging his head beneath the water spray.

"What isn't?"

"I finally get you naked, and within reach, and my body couldn't be any more tired if I was dead."

I chuckled and stepped forward, wrapping my arms around

his waist and pressing my naked body to his back. "I just want you to know I'm here for you."

And reassure myself that he was alive and well.

He'd buried a lot of pack members today, and I was so grateful that he hadn't been one of them.

CHAPTER 14
GALEN

My cock wanted to stir, but my body was so hurt, and my heart so broken after the burial task today, there was nothing left in me to respond to Talia the way she deserved.

"I'm so sorry." She pressed her lips against my back, her breasts caressing me from behind.

I sighed and closed my eyes, enjoying the feeling of her there. Her presence was comforting in a way I hadn't realized I needed.

Today had been so much harder than I'd ever thought a day could be. Watching the pack and the witches come together last night to fight as one had been inspiring, but seeing the grief-stricken souls today as we buried our dead and fought to keep the injured alive... It had taken every bit of my strength not to cry in front of everyone.

I was the Alpha, in the absence of my father, and they were all looking to me to provide a strong lead.

"Thank you," I said, my voice husky from holding everything in. "For looking after my dad. For keeping the children and the women safe."

It had been a brilliant move to bring all those who couldn't fight into my dad's protected house. There was strength in numbers, and the wards over this property made it the safest place in the whole pack territory.

"I was just glad I could help," she whispered, her words tickling the skin of my back.

I lifted my head and moved beneath the spray, rallying enough energy to scrub my face and hair. I was covered in filth. Dirt from the graves I'd dug, blood from those I'd carried.

I wouldn't go to bed tonight with the reminder still engrained on my body, but I would carry the memories forever in my heart.

Talia soaped my shoulders and down the backs of my arms.

"Could I have that?" I asked.

She smiled; I practically felt her lips lift upward. "Turn around and I'll do your front."

I was almost afraid to do as she asked. I didn't want to disappoint her.

"I..."

"Galen, just turn around. I'm only here to comfort you, not to put any pressure on you. Don't worry."

I forced back the fear and did as she asked, relief filling me when I saw no censure or disappointment in her expression. Instead, she simply grinned at me and began to wash my chest and belly in slow circles. I smiled down at her, enjoying the experience as calm washed over me.

"You know you have an Alpha edge to your voice sometimes," I told her. I hadn't heard it in many females. "My mom had it."

She'd been born an Alpha mate. But then, so had Talia.

She shrugged. "I just want what's best for you and sometimes you're stubborn, so I need to be firm."

Spoken like a true leader.

When her hands headed below my waist, I reached for the soap. "I can do the rest."

Her gaze flicked up at me through her long eyelashes. "Could I?"

Oh, God. Was this the right moment for that? But I wanted her. Badly.

"If you'd like to."

I thought she'd hurry through it embarrassed, or shy. But she didn't. She lathered up her hands with lots of soap, then ran her fingers up and down my cock, before exploring my balls, one at a time.

I SHOULDN'T HAVE FOUND her ministrations so arousing. They should have felt clinical, her explorations tentative.

But the more she cleaned me, the more the distress of the day fell away and the pleasure of her touch shone through.

My cock stirred and began to harden, finally waking from its temporary stasis. "I think it's time we took this to the bedroom."

Her gaze shot up, her eyes wide and a little hesitant—a look I was getting used to from her.

"Oh... ah..."

I grinned as I turned off the taps. "I have an idea. Do you trust me?"

She nodded, something that made every Alpha inch of me crow with pride. "Then let's go, beautiful one."

I reached around her hip and playfully tapped her on her

deliciously curvaceous ass. She squeaked a little, then jumped out of the shower cubicle and grabbed a towel for each of us.

I dried myself and waited as she did the same more slowly, then took her hand and led her to the bed. "I know you're a virgin and would prefer to be mated before you do anything too serious."

"Oh, um…"

"But there's lots of things we can do to pleasure each other that don't include taking your virginity."

I had a million little things I wanted to do with her.

She halted, and her face betrayed all sorts of emotions. Most of them not happy.

"But if you don't want to, I'll just go set up for a nap on the couch," I told her.

After all, it was still daytime, and she wasn't my mate.

"I'd, um… yes."

I frowned at her in confusion. "Yes. What? You want me to go set up on the couch for a nap?"

I hoped she didn't mean that, but I would definitely do it if she wanted me to. The last thing I would ever do was force any woman, let alone a virgin, into anything, even a kiss. Everything with Talia was forbidden, and sacred at the same time.

"Yes. I'd like to try some things. If that's okay?"

Okay? Hell yes it was okay!

I swung her up into my arms, loving the feel of her clean, naked body against my chest. She stared up at me with adoration and trust.

Now I had to find the strength not to make love to her the way I wanted to.

I placed her down on the bed and pulled out a bottle of the lube I kept in the top drawer.

"I want to touch you, is that okay?" I set the lube on the nightstand.

She lay on her back, shivering a little, and nodded.

I climbed onto the bed with her and slid under the covers, where she joined me in the warmth.

Today had been terrible, and a part of me really needed this affirmation of life. Another part just wanted Talia, plain and simple.

I turned toward her and gripped her waist. She wasn't moving, and her naiveté stalled me. I took a breath.

"Kiss me," I said, needing her to give me that last inch of permission before I showed her what pleasure could be found in a bed.

Her beautiful little nipples caught my attention as she turned to face me. She lifted her chin for my kiss.

It was all I needed. I grabbed her face and kissed her, feeling her warmth, her breath. I wanted to breathe life into the fire of the passion that was building slowly between us.

She moaned and kissed me back, grabbing my arms, clinging to me so tight I felt the twinge of her nails in my flesh.

I slid closer and began an exploration of her body with my hands and fingers. Her breasts were full and soft, filling my palm and making my cock swell further.

She moaned and moved forward, pressing her thighs into me.

I slid my palm into the indent of her waist and over her hip. She shifted, opening her legs a little.

I pushed her back so I could kiss her more easily. Then I grabbed the lube and squeezed some on my fingers. I wanted to make sure I didn't hurt her.

"Can I have some too?" she asked.

I didn't ask why. I was already too horny to speak at the

thought of touching her virginal body. I just did what she asked, squirting liquid into her palm before sliding my hand between her thighs.

She moaned and gasped at the first contact of my fingers against her already swollen clit, bucking a little as if she wanted more.

The groan that ripped from my throat was feral, but she answered with another moan that shivered all the way down to my wolf.

I circled her clit with my fingertips, then slid a single finger down between her lips to feel the entrance to her body.

She was wet and open, and as I slowly slid my finger into her tight, warm body, she wrapped her hand around my cock.

Pleasure burst through me and we groaned in unison, the air around us filling with the sounds of our mutual desire.

I kissed her deeper, harder, and moved my hand on her, alternating between pressing on her clit and exploring the depths of her perfect pussy.

She slid her hand up and down me, squeezing occasionally, then holding onto the head as she bucked and gasped on my fingers.

When she arched her back and her pussy tightened around my finger, I knew she was going to cum. My own orgasm had been teasing me, but I'd managed to keep it under control. Just.

But as she cried out and rippled around my fingers, my control slipped and the heat of my desire for her was torn from my body.

I came between her fingers while she came on my hand, and I claimed her mouth with the longest, hottest kiss of my life.

When the heat between us eventually died down, and the

ripples of pleasure subsided, I slid my hand out from between her legs and stared down at her awestruck eyes.

"You okay?"

She nodded, swallowing hard. "That was amazing."

I agreed, but there was a strange fullness in my heart—in that place where the heat of my passion for Talia had chased away the shadows. Then reality intruded and the shadows began to return.

"Shall we shower quickly?" I asked her, wanting to get up and reaching for the best excuse. "I've made a bit of a mess."

She reached for one of our discarded shower towels, wiped her hands, and then folded it over the wet spot.

"Let's have a sleep. I feel so... relaxed." She rolled onto her side and closed her eyes, the bliss of post-orgasm pleasure stealing over her.

"Let me just go to the bathroom. I'll be back." I kissed her lips, rolled out of bed, then stopped to tuck her in before I went to clean up.

When I looked in the mirror, the churning emotions inside me were obvious in my expression. Had Talia seen that, before she fell asleep? I hoped not. She didn't deserve that. But the darkness was back, along with the doubts, even though I didn't want to acknowledge them. Being with Talia had been too good. I'd felt things I'd never felt, and other things I hadn't experienced for far too long.

Jessie.

What had happened to her had followed me through the years. I couldn't go through that again. Losing the girl I loved had almost killed me.

Which meant getting close to a woman like Talia was dangerous, and that meant I needed to be more careful about guarding my heart.

And other parts of my body that seemed too eager to love her.

I crept back into my old bedroom and stared down at her. She was fast asleep. A huge part of me ached to climb back beneath the blankets and curl into her, reveling in her warmth and light.

But I couldn't.

I grabbed some clean clothes, dressed quickly, and went to see my dad. After all, I had a lot to report.

CHAPTER 15
TALIA

Waking up in the middle of the day was such a strange experience. I was disorientated for a minute, then I realized where I was. And why I was naked.

The memories of what Galen and I had done came flooding back, as did the feelings of complete exhilaration.

I rolled onto my back, tugged the blankets up to my face, and bit down on the sheets to stop the squeal from emerging.

Galen had been so incredibly thoughtful. And talented. And hot!

Hearing him groan as he came had made my own orgasm so much more intense.

Speaking of Galen... where was he?

I sat up in bed and glanced around the room, listening for anyone in the bathroom or the hallway outside the bedroom. Silence. How long had I been asleep?

I stretched out my hand to stroke the indented spot next to me on the bed. The space that Galen had occupied for a short, hot time this afternoon.

It was cold.

I must have been asleep far longer than expected, for him to have left me alone so long.

I slid out of bed and hurried to the bathroom for a shower. I dressed quickly, wanting to go and find Galen. The sun was low in the sky which meant it must be close to dinner time by now.

I rushed out of my room and found Max asleep in his room, and no sign of Galen anywhere.

Where was he?

I went into the kitchen and began the preparations for dinner. There was a basket of homemade bread sitting on the counter, delivered yesterday by one of the other pack women prior to the battle, and I figured the bread would go nicely with steak and a salad. I grabbed a knife and salad ingredients from the fridge and began to chop.

Was the battle really only last night? It felt like so much had happened since then—my sexy afternoon sojourn with Galen chief among them.

I was lucky my shifter genes had enabled my injuries to heal so quickly. I still had twinges in my chest from my ribs, but the pain was reduced to a dull ache that I could tolerate, and I hadn't even thought about them while in bed with Galen.

I still couldn't believe I had fought off Maddox. A frown marred my face. Nor that so many of Galen's pack had been injured or killed.

I felt a little out of whack due to being up most of the night, then sleeping twice during the day.

My emotions seemed a little bit all over the place, though I supposed there was a good enough reason to feel as if I were on a rollercoaster. The truth was, I felt a little dizzy. I drank a large glass of water and took a deep breath, raising my gaze to look out the kitchen window and try to center myself.

Outside in the street, pack members trudged up and down in front of the house.

An older man limped down the road, children surrounding him in support. A woman carried a basket of food, but her eye was cut and her face badly bruised. Another woman walked by, her left arm bent strangely as she hugged it into her chest. The signs of damage that my old pack had done to these beautiful people were all around me.

I dropped the knife to the countertop, my fingers tightening into fists. Fucking Maddox and his fucking Alpha father. All this hatred and death. And for what?

Pack lands?

More of what they already had?

They didn't even need more land.

"Fucking... Maddox!"

I picked up the knife, then slammed it down again on the countertop, unable to contain my anger. If they hadn't attacked Galen's pack in the first place, they wouldn't have lost.

My father wouldn't have made some 'mistake'.

He wouldn't have been murdered by the Alpha he loved, and to whom he had always remained loyal, no matter what.

And I wouldn't have been rejected by my mate and tossed away like trash.

No.

It was far worse than that. I'd been thrown away, then hunted down to be killed.

And all these lovely people from Galen's pack, who had been so welcoming to me, wouldn't now be dead, injured, or suffering.

No matter what happened, they didn't seem able to leave me alone. Even after they'd failed. Even after Galen beat their Alpha and made a deal with them to lay the hell off and stay clear of our pack and lands. Galen's people didn't deserve what had happened to them, and neither did I.

I pushed off from the kitchen counter and marched along the hallway, then turned and paced back just as forcefully. I didn't know what to do with all these feelings. I wanted to yell, and scream, and fight that bastard Maddox all over again.

This time, I wouldn't stop until I'd torn out his throat.

I wanted vengeance for my father.

For all the victims of Maddox and his asshole father.

And I wanted vengeance for myself. For the old life I'd lost. For the burgeoning new life here in Galen's pack that they'd tried to take, and failed.

I was so angry, my wolf began to howl, deep down inside me. She wanted to shift and tear things apart with her teeth.

"Talia!" Max called out, pulling me back to the here and now. "You okay?"

I strode to his room, still breathing hard, trying and only just managing to contain my rage. I kept my wolf tucked away.

"Yeah." My tone was gruff. It didn't sound like me. "I was just making dinner. Shouldn't take too long, if you're hungry."

He stared at me, blinking a few times as he took in my new sense of purpose. "You don't look like yourself, Talia. Are you sure you're all right?"

I crossed my arms over my chest and stood in the doorway, staring at the Alpha who'd given me leave to call him by his first name.

"No, Max, I'm not all right. I—"

"You're angry."

I nodded at him. "Hell yes, I am. My old pack... what they've done to yours and Galen's people. I'm so angry at them. I'm enraged."

My whole body was shaking.

He grinned at me with a flash of teeth and a gleam of the old wolf in his dark eyes. "Good. Hold onto that rage, my dear. Tamp it down but keep it ready. That's what you'll need to beat them."

A strange type of happiness filled me up seeing Max display the strength that I knew was there beneath the surface of his illness.

I opened my mouth to say something positive along those lines.

A massive crash erupted at the other end of the hallway.

I turned toward the sound and called out, "Who's there?"

There was a whisper of heat on the breeze, but no one answered.

Hairs rose up on the back of my neck and dread trickled all the way down my spine.

I knew, deep down in my gut, that this intruder was no ordinary wolf shifter.

I exchanged a quick look with Max, and then ran out into the hallway, holding my anger ready to fuel a burst of energy, just as he had advised.

You'll need your rage to beat them.

There was no one in sight, but another thump in one of the rooms down the hall signaled the truth. Someone had broken into our house, knocking through our wards.

And I had the strangest sense that, whoever it was, they had come here just for me.

THE END... continued in Wolf of Shadows: HERE

Printed in Great Britain
by Amazon